MANTRAP!

The trail looped back close to the river and led into a stretch of pine tree country.

"Look lively," Dan'l warned his companions as he urged his horse forward to take the point. "Ambush country. Check your loads, make sure your powder ain't clumped."

And perhaps because he was looking for a strike from their distant flanks, Dan'l became a mite too complacent about the trail immediately before them. The carpeting of pine needles had grown even thicker, completely covering the sod.

His horse, moving forward at a steady trot, planted his left forefoot, then suddenly pitched hard toward the ground. Dan'l's very first thought was that the animal had stepped into a gopher hole.

But this "hole," Dan'l quickly realized when *both* the horse's forelegs were swallowed up, was a man-made pitfall trap! The pine-needle-covered framework of boughs collapsed, and Dan'l pitched forward over his pommel— straight toward three pointed stakes smeared black with deadly poison!

The *Dan'l Boone: The Lost Wilderness Tales* series:

DAN'L BOONE
BY HONOR BOUND

DODGE TYLER

LEISURE BOOKS NEW YORK CITY

Dedicated to a modern-day Dan'l,
Frank Joseph Soss, Jr.

A LEISURE BOOK®

July 1999

Published by

Dorchester Publishing Co., Inc.
276 Fifth Avenue
New York, NY 10001

ISBN 0-8439-4559-1

Printed in the United States of America.

BY HONOR BOUND

Chapter One

"Looks to me," said young Evan Blackford, "like we finally got us a *nation* shaping up, Dan'l! Leastways, if we ever get shut of them English devils, we'll have us a nation."

"We'll get shut of John Bull," Dan'l replied confidently. "No misdoubting that. Sure as the Lord made Moses, this land *will* pass to our children's children. But it won't come easy. Right now there's too many pigs and too few teats."

Even as he said this in his easygoing mountaineer's drawl, Dan'l's clear, deep-set, penetrating eyes stayed in constant motion, scanning the forest to either side of the pike in search of trouble. The two men, dressed in the butternut-dyed uniforms of the newly formed

7

Kentucky Militia, rode abreast. Within hailing distance behind them, Dan'l's oldest son, Israel, drove Becky and the rest of the Boone tribe in a new surrey.

"I *still* don't credit the news," Evan said. "After all them threats and foreclosures, now Governor Hammond just up and agrees to recognize any duly filed land warrant. I wish—"

The lad's throat abruptly tightened on him, and he fell silent for a moment. Dan'l knew Evan was thinking about that terrible day, almost a year ago now, when the rest of the Blackford family had been brutally massacred at Blackford's Mill by the Shawnee and Fox tribes.

"I wish Ma and Pa coulda lived to see this day," Evan resumed. "Blackford's Mill not only thriving again, but now about to become part of the Colony of Virginia. A by-God charter, Dan'l! No more frets about some greedy land company taking title to our property and pushing us out."

Dan'l nodded. "Looks that way, anyhow," he said carefully. "But we best not start spending ahead of the harvest. Promises been made before, too. Turned out they was writ on water."

When it came to highly coveted land titles, in this heady decade of the 1770's, Dan'l knew that rumors were always thicker than toads after a hard rain. But finally, the pioneer-hating Lord Dunmore had been called back to London by the Colonial Secretary. Now Virginia Colony had a halfway decent governor in Cornelius Hammond. Hammond tried to balance his loyalty to England against his sympathy for colonial pioneers.

And Hammond had offered the far-flung, trans-Appalachian settlers of Boonesborough, Harrodsburg, and other frontier settlements an enticing arrangement: He would recognize all duly filed land warrants. The settlers, in turn, must agree to organize Kentucky as part of the Colony of Virginia and to provide for the common defense of the entire colony.

And thus, this very day there was to be a double celebration at the parade commons—a truly grand gala. The new Kentucky Militia, under command of Major Daniel Boone, was to be officially commissioned. And then, before a secular feast began, the deeply religious Kaintucks meant to give heartfelt thanks to the Lord Almighty for His divine providence. It looked like this was *their* land at long last!

"Why, Dan'l!" Evan's voice sliced into Dan'l's pleasant rumination. "Your horse has gone lame!"

Boone grinned wide, and strong white teeth flashed out of a square, sun-weathered face that was presently smooth-shaven—a sure sign Dan'l had not been yondering lately. He only shaved when he was in the settlements, as required by law.

"Lame, huh?" he said. "Which foot?"

"Why . . . the right forefoot—see him favor it?"

"Uh-huh, I see it. You just wait a bit. Next, it'll

be the left hindfoot. He's foolin' us, ain'tcha, Rip?"

Young Evan removed his tricorn hat to scratch his head. The youth was slight of build and as dark as an Indian. He cut a proud figure in his new uniform, but was still so young that down covered his cheeks.

Evan stared at Rip. Dan'l's favorite horse was an ugly, dish-faced ginger—a sturdy little fifteen-hand descendant of Southwest mustang stock Dan'l himself had driven back east from the Wild Horse Desert of New Spain.

Dan'l laughed at the dubious look in the lad's eyes.

"When it comes to horses, sprout, never let appearances be your guide. A pretty horse is a petted horse, and a petted horse is spoiled. Now, thissen's ugly as a heath witch. But *fast*? Well, I reckon! Why, happen I should spur him right now, he'd light out like Going was his ma's name and Fast his pa's. And as you see—he's smart enough to fake lameness to avoid duty!"

Dan'l dropped back to check on his family. There was a hubcap missing off the surrey. But in honor of this day, there was fresh blacking on the dashboard and a new whip in the socket.

Becky, her face framed in golden curls, smiled at her husband from under a calico sunbonnet.

"Major Boone!" she called out gaily. "Thee has a rebellion on thy hands! Tell thy son here he's still too young to go soldiering."

Becky, like Dan'l, had lapsed somewhat in her

strict Quaker training. But she always switched to the formality of "First Day" or Sunday speech on important occasions such as today.

Dan'l glanced at the scowling Israel. The fifteen-year-old was big and strapping for his age, and already had his father's determined eye and stalwart jaw.

"Ain't fair," Israel complained. "When you was only sixteen, Pa, you went off by yourself on your first long hunt! I'm bigger 'n Evan, and he's only two years older than me. But *he* can go for a soldier—a officer, at that."

Dan'l understood the boy's frustration. But Boone had already lost his son James only three years earlier during an Indian attack in the Cumberland Gap. He had no desire to molly-coddle this boy, but losing a child was a deeper hurt than any arrow point or bullet could inflict. Dan'l wasn't eager to feel it again.

"You'll go for a soldier, son," Dan'l assured him. "There'll be no shortage of scrapes and battles, and you'll get your fill of them. The world ain't likely to grow honest anytime soon. But your ma and sisters need a stout man to home when I can't be there. Your pa sleeps easier knowing Israel Boone is up and on the line."

A stout man! This praise from his father swelled Israel with pride. He sat up a little straighter behind the reins and squared his shoulders.

"Papa!" called out little Jemima from the back seat. "There's something on your face!"

Dan'l grinned, for it was a familiar little game between them.

"Oh, Lord, no," he said with mock chagrin, leaning his face close to the little girl's. "What *is* it?"

"A *kiss*!" she shouted, laughing with delight as she planted one on Dan'l's cheek.

Dan'l and Becky laughed, too, and Dan'l tousled the girl's hair. Then he clucked to his horse and joined Evan again.

"Fine day, ain't it, Major Boone?" Evan said.

"Still got the Lord's thumbprint fresh on it, Lieutenant Blackford," Dan'l agreed, looking around them with satisfaction. Spring had come roaring in recently, and now the fox grapes and wild mint flourished. The trees were swollen with new sap, and long fingers of sunlight revealed the silvery flash-and-dart of minnows in the nearby Kentucky River. Now and then Dan'l heard fat bass plopping in the deeper pools.

It was a scene out of a storybook. But Dan'l never confused stories with life. That was why he was immediately alert when he heard the sudden hooting of an owl.

"What's the matter?" Evan asked, seeing his commander suddenly rein in and stare off into the shadowy depths of the forest.

"Mayhap it ain't nothing," Dan'l finally replied. "You hear that owl?"

"Naw. But so what? Owls *live* in the woods."

"For a fact they do," Dan'l replied, squeezing Rip with his knees to start him forward again.

"But they generally hole up by day and hunt by night."

"This one could be notional," Evan suggested.

"Ahuh. Mayhap 'notional' is the very word," Dan'l agreed absently.

Take a good look, Sheltowee. Your death-bringer has arrived.

The Shawnee renegade named War Hawk was perched high in a silver spruce overlooking the Boonesborough Pike. Below him rode the whiteskin legend who had become the greatest enemy, white or red, of the Shawnee tribe: Daniel Boone to his own people, Sheltowee to the outraged, and now permanently displaced, Shawnees.

War Hawk wore an eagle-bone whistle thrust into his greasy topknot. He was tall and well muscled for an Indian, his pox-scarred face sharp-featured like a fox's. And now, eyes like black agates watched Boone as rage transformed War Hawk's visage into a mask of violent hatred.

This was the man War Hawk had vowed, in front of all his people, to kill and scalp. That was War Hawk's right. For it was his band that had captured Boone while he was making salt near the Clinch River settlement.

But instead, Boone had escaped, making a fool out of War Hawk, turning him into a squaw in front of his own tribe!

Yes, there had been some satisfactions for the Shawnee tribe. One of Boone's children killed at Cumberland Gap, Boone's brother Edward killed during attacks in Ohio. And only one winter ago, War Hawk himself had personally slaughtered two families in Boonesborough, both of them very dear friends of the mighty Sheltowee.

But the Shawnee list of grievances was long and bitter. Twice Boone had managed to escape from them. Another time, he had led the rescue of his daughter and several other whiteskin girls held captive by the Shawnees. However, most galling of all: It was Boone's brilliant Indian-fighting campaigns that had permanently driven the Shawnees from their ancestral homeland.

Now, against their will, War Hawk and his people had wandered far to the north and west, well beyond the river called Great Waters.

Regretfully, War Hawk knew he would never return permanently to these eastern lands. For he had tasted the waters of Manitou, and Ute legend said it would always call him back, the eternal wanderer.

No. He had come this long way for one purpose only: to avenge himself in the eyes of his people, to make Daniel Boone die hard. As hard as a man could die.

War Hawk's sun-slitted eyes flicked left, to the surrey following Boone and the young buck. The woman's yellow hair seemed to have trapped the very light of the sun itself.

Boone could only die once, no matter how hard War Hawk made the dying. But a loving husband and father died many times over when his family went under before he did.

Again War Hawk cupped his hands before his mouth and expertly imitated an owl hooting. He wanted Boone to know, yet *not* know—to *feel* death everywhere, yet *see* it nowhere.

"The end will finally come, Sheltowee," he vowed out loud. "All that remains for you is the dying!"

Chapter Two

"Eyes . . . right!"

Lieutenant Evan Blackford, marching proudly at the head of the new, one-hundred-man-strong Kentucky County Militia, barked out the command as two platoons of soldiers passed the reviewing stand.

Major Boone stood solid as a meetinghouse at the front of the stand. He saluted back, and when he did, a six-pounder cannon roared out. A resounding cheer went up from hundreds of spectators scattered about the parade commons.

Sharing the new pine reviewing stand with Dan'l were all the area's dignitaries. These included Josiah Burns, the circuit judge; Septimus Luce, the Kaintucks' new representative to the Virginia House of Burgesses; and Reverend Lemuel Perkins.

When the military review was complete, and the militiamen stood at parade rest with their muskets and flintlock rifles, Reverend Perkins came forward to lead the settlers in prayer.

A respectful hush descended over the crowd. Even though most of the Kaintucks were Quakers, Lemuel was exceedingly well liked despite being a Methodist—and one who tended toward the "shouting order" at that.

"Almighty God!" he roared out, and had they been indoors, his powerful voice would have shaken the building. "Your children are gathered here today in your sight to give humble thanks. We thank you first for this bountiful land, which finally, at long last, will be secured to us under secular law and title.

"We thank you, too, for men the likes of Daniel Boone and these courageous volunteers of his who have pledged their very lives, in your holy name, to defend our new homeland. Lord, there's still a lot of work to be done for all of us. But God willing, we'll *get* it done! Amen."

A heartfelt "Amen!" from the onlookers was followed by another booming cannon roar. Then the frock-coated Septimus Luce came forward. He placed a monocle in his right eye so he could see the crowd better.

"Fellow Kaintucks!" he roared out. "As you all know by now, unless you've been trapped in a badger hole these last weeks, Governor Hammond has agreed to validate all duly filed land warrants in the Cumberland Plateau and Appalachian Highlands."

More raucous cheers. Hats flew into the air, and a few muskets were discharged.

"I thought," Luce continued, pulling a folded quarto sheet out from his inside coat pocket, "that you might like to hear this. These words were written by a distinguished editorialist in Rowan County, North Carolina. They describe the man we have placed in charge of protecting our women, our children, our very homes."

Luce gave his talk a pulpit pause. A profound hush settled over the sun-drenched parade commons. It was so quiet that all assembled could hear the bird chatter from the surrounding forest. Then Luce began reading in a strong, clear voice:

"Daniel Boone has that rarest of knacks—a skill vastly unrelated to hunting or exploring or warring. Boone's vision cuts through the vast differences of our still-divided population and expresses the common sentiment. He binds us one to another as entirely new creatures called 'Americans.' Boone voices what might best be called the national sentiment that is uniquely *ours*, not England's!"

These words caused a veritable explosion of cheers and whistles. Dan'l could see Becky near the front of the pressing crowd, tears of pride and happiness rolling across her fair cheeks.

It was a triumphant moment, and Dan'l tried hard to share in the common mood of joyful celebration. But those almost-mocking owl hoots from earlier were still with him, rankling at him like burrs under a saddle blanket. Especially because Dan'l knew the owl hoot was a common signal among the tribe that hated him most, the Shawnees.

Again Dan'l's eyes cut to the surrounding trees, and fear tickled his belly.

"Some of the Indians in that region," Enis Birdwell said, "even believe Boone is immortal and cannot be killed. Some of them are actually too afraid of him to even try to kill him. That's precisely what results when ignorant mountain rabble and godless savages are allowed off their leash."

Birdwell, Revenue Officer for the Colony of Virginia, sat behind a huge scrollwork desk. He was big, soft, and pear-shaped, with shrewd eyes in a fleshy face. His powdered wig was hardly more pale than his complexion.

"But the mighty long hunter does not yet realize," Birdwell continued in his precise, nasal voice, "that Governor Hammond has been called back to the mother country. And in the Governor's long absence, *I* am the highest legal authority concerning matters of land claims."

Birdwell picked up a quill pen made from a goose feather and dipped it in a pot of ink, then began to write something on a sheet of fancy foolscap. The man across the desk from him, John "Big Sandy" Lavoy, watched his superior with curious, amused eyes. Lavoy was built large, like his employer, but there was no soft place on—or inside—him.

"I want you to deliver this proclamation to Septimus Luce in Boonesborough," Birdwell continued. "I'll also make copies for Boone and some others. It doesn't really matter if Boone is 'immortal.' I can take something even more valuable than his life—I can take his *land*."

Birdwell finished writing and blotted the sheet with sand. Before he sealed it with wax, he let Big Sandy read it.

"To all who shall read these words, greetings! Be it known that numerous violations of King George's Proclamation Act of 1763 have resulted in official repudiation of *all* land claims west of the Allegheny Mountains."

Big Sandy looked up at his employer and whistled in surprise. The much-despised Proclamation Act, forbidding settlement of the transmontane wilderness, had never really been enforceable. Big Sandy resumed reading.

"All settlement in this disputed region is retroactively illegal as of this date. By the standard terms of land repudiation, all settlers have sixty days to legally secure their claims by paying one dollar per acre. Those who pay will be granted clear titles immediately. Those who do not will be evicted and the land placed on sale to the first bidders."

Big Sandy flashed a lopsided grin and handed the notice back to his boss so he could seal it. "I wonder who those 'first bidders' might be."

Birdwell grinned back, his big, fleshy nose

wrinkling at the bridge. "Fortune favors the bold, Sandy. Keep up your good services for me, and *you* will settle in Boone's own cabin if you like."

Birdwell was convinced he was bound for greatness if only he could control the confounding forces arrayed against him—chief among them being Daniel Boone. In point of fact, Birdwell had risen to power by being far more importunate than deserving. He possessed a real skill at disguising his criminal deceit behind a cloak of patriotism.

Birdwell had learned early on in this neophyte nation that it was far easier to profit off the work and risks of others than to break a sweat yourself. Thus, he had become a master of the "great commoner" act. The eloquence of a prophet disguised a base profiteer's dishonesty.

Big Sandy said, "They'll never raise the money. Not in sixty days."

"Not by a jugful," Birdwell agreed. "Therein lies the beauty of it. As you know, I am a barrister by profession, trained in common law at the King's Court in London. I have already begun the legal incorporation of a charter for the Kentucky Land Company. That charter already lists dozens of claimants. And by a stroke of good fortune, they are all my indentured workers."

"You mean . . . your tobacco plantation workers?"

Birdwell nodded, tucking a pinch of snuff

into his cheek. "Precisely. Although most don't realize it. It was a proviso buried deep in their indenture agreements—all have agreed they will sell these holdings to me at a penny per acre."

"How much land are we talking about?" Big Sandy asked.

"About twenty thousand acres of the best soil in the western lands," Birdwell replied. "Soil so rich, you can leave your hoe stuck in the ground overnight, and there'll be grapes growing on the handle by morning!"

Big Sandy loosed another whistle. "Good God a-gorry! So the Kaintucks would have to raise twenty thousand dollars in sixty days? Why, horses will mate with bears first."

That sum, in the 1770's, was absolutely staggering. Especially in a country where hard currency was scarce and most folks still did business by barter and trade.

Birdwell smiled as he flicked a speck of snuff off his sleeve. "Exactly. As I said—we won't even worry about Boone's 'immortality.' *Let* him live forever and savor his misery while he does! I assure you, the arrogant rustic bastard won't be doing it in Kentucky."

Chapter Three

Eight days after Birdwell and Lavoy's fateful meeting in Richmond, Dan'l found a crow feather lying only ten feet from the door of the Boone cabin.

At first, Dan'l stood staring at the black feather for a full minute.

Crow feathers . . . black symbolized death, and one was added to a Shawnee's war bonnet for every scalp taken. But *was* this a sign? Crows were not common in these wooded areas, preferring the open fields and meadows beyond the common square. But neither was it impossible that one might stray in, searching for food.

Dan'l realized this was just like that owl hoot he'd heard—a sign that wasn't clearly a sign at all. As if someone were playing a fear game with him. Someone cunning like the Shawnee battle leader, War Hawk.

"Could just be happen-chance," Dan'l muttered to himself. Still, fearful ideas were popping in his mind like fireworks. No, it was nothing he could easily lay his tongue to—a feeling more than a certainty.

After finding the feather, Dan'l went back inside the split-log cabin, still wondering. There were three big rooms with a wide sleeping loft and a lean-to for storage. The inside was neatly whitewashed, with new puncheon floors, solid chinking, a sturdy clapboard roof, and a dry, clean cellar—this last being a true luxury on the frontier. It also concealed a secret escape tunnel in case of Indian attack.

"What is it?" Becky asked, catching sight of Dan'l's preoccupied face. She dropped another dumpling into a pot of beans. In a corner behind the Franklin stove, corn cobs soaked in a bucket of coal oil—quick-cooking fuel when wood was wet or time scarce. A hot huckleberry cobbler was cooling on the windowsill.

"Mayhap nothing," Dan'l assured his wife, lifting his broad-brimmed hat from its peg beside the door. Dan'l also took his flintlock breechloader down from the rack and shook fresh powder into the frizzen.

He brushed his lips across the back of Becky's neck—her kitchen-warmed skin smelled of sweet lavender. "Think I'll saddle Rip and ride out to Blackford's Mill, see how Evan is doing."

Becky was no coward, and Dan'l would take her into his confidence the moment he was sure that War Hawk had returned. But the first person who had a right to know was young Evan Blackford. The last time War Hawk had ventured this way, Evan's entire family had paid the price. Besides, young or no, Evan was next in command of the militia. He had to be told.

Now a fearful Dan'l wondered: Was the Boone family next on War Hawk's bloody list?

Dan'l made the four-mile ride to Blackford's Mill in jig time. He quickly explained his growing suspicion to the young officer, then both men rode out toward the gravel ford on Dick's River—home of the area's most venerable and knowledgeable Indian-fighter, Brendan "Jip" Adair.

The two friends found the old-timer cleaning fish on a stump in front of his hovel beside the river.

"Hallo, old roadster!" Dan'l greeted him.

"Light down, Sheltowee!" the trapper replied, raising a knife that glittered with fish scales. "Ain't seed you in a coon's age!"

The two riders dismounted and loosed their saddle cinches. Then they slipped their bits and threw their bridles, leading their horses to the river to drink. It was a fine day, birds twittering in the nearby woods, mud daubers skimming drunkenly along the river's glassy surface.

Old Jip was of big-boned Ulster stock, the same breed of hearty Irish males who would eventually fill the ranks of a new nation's army and police forces. He was weathered brown as an acorn, his clothes as greasy as his shoulder-length gray hair. Dan'l noticed he wore three pair of trousers, only one of which hadn't gone through at the knees. Jip didn't know his exact age, but Dan'l figured the old frontiersman for at least sixty.

Jip stared at Evan, who wore his military forage cap.

"Militia!" Jip spat scornfully. Everything men did was tarnal foolishness to him. Even the most remote frontier outpost was too damned civilized for Jip Adair. "Militia, my sweet aunt! Buncha boys with their pants in their boots! What's that womanish foforaw doin' on your conk cover?"

Jip meant the gold piping Evan had sewn onto his cap.

The lad flushed. To Evan's youthful eye, the old man looked to be straight out of Genesis. "It sets me off as a officer," Evan explained.

Jip spat again. "Huh! A damned popish dido is what it is."

Evan's embarrassment flared into quick anger. But Jip suddenly laughed and slapped the boy on one shoulder. "Ahh, I'm just twitting you, tadpole. Come down off your hind legs! You may be green on the antlers, but the Blackford men have less fear in 'em than a rifle! So what's on the spit, boys?"

Dan'l showed Jip the crow feather and mentioned the almost mocking owl hoots he'd heard last week in broad daylight.

"I'm thinkin' mayhap War Hawk is back," Dan'l concluded. "He made his boast that he would be."

Jip mulled all this while he scooped out handfuls of fish guts and tossed them to two old hunting dogs. It was natural that Dan'l would seek his old friend's counsel on matters concerning red men. Jip had spent years as an itinerant trader among the tribes, had even taken an Indian wife who'd later died of childbed fever. He was fluent in several Indian dialects, knew sign talk, and was familiar with the red man's customs and thinking.

"Iffen War Hawk's back," Jip finally said, "I ain't heard nothing in the drums about it. But say! I hope there *is* trouble, goddamnit! I'm sick o' this placid, punkin-butter existence. Let's wake snakes, Boone, like we done in the old days!"

"Old days be hanged. We don't need Indian trouble," Dan'l insisted.

"Ah, you're apron-tied, Boone! Course, it's one peart-lookin' gal wearin' the apron, so's I can't rightly fault ye. You got a good woman, Dan boy."

"And mean to *keep* her," Dan'l shot back. But he felt a stab of guilt at the pain these words obviously caused Evan—the boy had lost all to savages.

Before they could return to the topic of War Hawk, Dan'l heard a horse approaching from the east. The rider broke clear of the trees near the river, a big, fair-skinned stranger on a seventeen-hand sorrel.

The man was about to spur his horse past the group of men. Then his face showed surprised recognition, and he reined in.

"Well, now, Daniel Boone! Timely met! I got somethin' here for you, Boone."

Dan'l squinted for a few moments, studying the man's hard, unpleasant face. "John Lavoy," he finally remembered out loud, not with any pleasure. The two men had met before, on opposite sides of a lively skirmish back in '67.

"My friends call me Big Sandy," Lavoy said.

"Good for them. I'll stick with Lavoy. State your business."

"With pleasure. Enis Birdwell asked me to deliver this," Lavoy said, smirking as he pulled a folded sheet of foolscap from his shirt. "Maybe the kid can read it to you, Boone. I read in Filson's book how the 'great' Daniel Boone has a hard go of it tryin' to read and write."

Lavoy's horse was prancing backward the moment Dan'l took the proclamation from him. The book Lavoy meant was John Filson's *The Adventures of Daniel Boone*, recently published.

"I also have copies for Judge Burns and Septimus Luce," Lavoy added. "So ignore this if you've a mind to, Boone. Don't matter. Your cake is dough now, famous man!"

As a matter of fact, Dan'l's formal learning *was* limited—the forest had been his classroom, and nature his tutor. But Squire Boone and

Sarah Morgan had made sure all their children could cipher and read book-lettering. Dan'l had no trouble understanding Birdwell's repudiation of the Kaintucks' land warrants.

"Evicted?" Evan demanded even as Lavoy's horse pounded out of sight. "Why, they can't do that! Can they, Dan'l? It ain't right!"

Dan'l was silent for a full minute, his eyes losing their focus as he considered this new disaster. Dan'l had learned the hard way that, on the contentious frontier, true justice had little to do with the raw power of crooked law.

"I caught rumors that Governor Hammond was called back to England," Dan'l finally said. He stared at the fateful notice. "But I didn't credit the stories. Looks like I was wrong."

Hot blood rushed to Evan's almost-beardless face. "Two months to raise one dollar for *each* goldang acre? Why, Dan'l! I'd need a hunnert and fifty dollars for my piece. The mill don't clear that much in a year! We got to call a meeting and tell the others!"

"No need to bother," Dan'l assured him. "This'll soon get noised about."

Jip snorted. "Noised about? Huh! They'll bawl like bay steers."

"I've heard this 'n' that about Birdwell," Dan'l said. "They say he'd steal dead flies from a blind spider."

"Aye, this coon's crossed trails with old Birdwell afore," Jip chimed in. His long Irish upper lip wrinkled in scorn. "That son of a bitch is shiftier than a creased buck."

"Well," Dan'l said, glancing at their lengthening shadows, "day's closing in. No sense chewing it fine right now. Let's make tracks, Evan."

But as they caught up their mounts, Dan'l realized the Kaintucks might well be pinned between the jaws of a powerful trap: War Hawk being one jaw, Enis Birdwell the other.

Leastways, Dan'l consoled himself, *there ain't no solid proof yet that War Hawk is back.* This new disaster with the land repudiation was serious enough. But as bad as it was, it paled in contrast to the threat from War Hawk.

Lord, Dan'l prayed, *keep that murdering renegade far hence from here.*

Only about a half hour of daylight remained by the time Big Sandy Lavoy had delivered all the copies of Birdwell's new proclamation.

Despite his bold effrontery toward Boone, Big Sandy wanted to get the hell away from the Kaintuck settlements as soon as possible. Once word got around that all these local rustics were being ousted, lead *would* fly. Plenty of it his way, too, if he didn't point bridle back toward Virginia.

To make better time, he stuck to the grassy bank of the Kentucky River. Big Sandy kept his eyes peeled for a good campsite near the water. He had no desire to ride after dark in this wild hill-and-holler country rife with mean bears and vicious wildcats.

His horse suddenly whinnied, and Big Sandy

dropped his right hand to the big German cap-and-ball dragon pistol in his sash.

However, he realized—his throat closing in sudden fear—that he was already too late. A half-naked Shawnee brave sat his mount directly in Big Sandy's path!

Then the relieved man realized this brave brandished no weapon. A moment later, despite the gathering darkness, Big Sandy recognized him.

"Well, cuss my coup! War Hawk! So you're still alive?"

"That, or you have seen a ghost. Many winters have passed us."

Big Sandy nodded. "For a fact. Been nine years now."

"As you say. And Boone still alive."

Big Sandy grinned. "Alive, but he may soon be naked. As landless and poor as Job's turkey."

Keeping it simple, Lavoy explained the new crisis Boone and the Kaintucks faced. These two men had joined forces, back in '67, in a nearly successful attempt to kill Boone along the Big Sandy River, Lavoy's namesake.

"I hope you do ruin him," War Hawk said. "Take his land *and* his manhood! But only if I fail to kill him."

"So that's why you're here? You mean to do for Boone?"

"I did not come this far to study the causes of the wind!"

Big Sandy nodded, a canny light sparking to life in his eyes. "Right now," he said, "Birdwell

31

wants to rein in a bit, see what Boone will do. But I'm thinking the boss will be glad to hear you're in this neck of the woods. Maybe you and me can both feather our nests if we throw in together again."

War Hawk turned this over for a few moments, examining all the facets. Finally he nodded. War Hawk knew how generous whiteskins could be when it came to payment for killing their enemies.

"Go speak with your chief," War Hawk said. "Find out his terms and tell them to me. I mean to kill Sheltowee, and the Wendigo himself will not stop me! But even better if Boone's death can make me rich."

Chapter Four

Old Jip was right—the Kaintucks did "bawl like bay steers" when news of Birdwell's land-repudiation notice spread through the area.

Even before a general meeting could be called, Nat Bischoff led a delegation of angry men to see Major Boone, head of the Kentucky Rifles. Dan'l took a visiting-jug of corn mash out into the yard and greeted each man by name. It was late afternoon, a hot yellow sun stuck high in the sky as if nailed there.

"Dan'l," Nat said in his thick Dutch accent, "it's a fine t'ing, by Gott, we formed a militia, heah? This gott-damned Birdwell must be filt with lead, the greedy piker!"

"Stow that militia 'n' lead talk," Dan'l advised easily. "This battle can be won by wit and wile."

Nat and several others erupted in protest. But the big, serene frontiersman patiently lifted both hands like a priest blessing his flock. They quieted down like Indians whose chief had crossed his arms for silence.

"Back in the early sixties," Dan'l reminded them, "we could afford some dustups hereabouts. *Had* us some, too, some real busters. But that was before we had so many womenfolk and little-uns living in the settlements. You boys ain't forest bachelors now. You eager to put your families at risk?"

That question settled the men down in a hurry. Dan'l wasn't the only man present who had lost family to Indians.

"A-course we ain't, Dan'l," replied Morgan Trapp. "But t'ain't fair! This cussed Enis Birdwell is telling us there ain't room in the pond but for one big frog. And *him* that frog!"

"We're all beholden to you, Dan'l," tossed in Graham Ahearn. "But that bastard Birdwell is evicting us from our own land!"

"You got it hindside foremost," Dan'l corrected him. "*We* are going to evict the likes of Birdwell. Forever. It won't be easy, but we can do 'er."

A few men scratched their chins and traded puzzle-headed glances at this.

"Dan'l," Morgan suggested tactfully. "You sound like them politicians when they's lectioneering. We—"

"Just hold your horses, Morgan," Dan'l cut in. "We can win this one, I'm saying. Grass can

34

push a stone right on over. It just needs time, is all."

"Time? Dan'l, my old ma needs time! Don't we all? But Birdwell gave us two months, is all. That's piddlin'!"

"Ahuh. Ain't much, but it's time enough. By the time the corn has leafed and come to full ear, this land will be ours forever. The whole shivaree!"

"How?" Nat demanded.

"We'll pay for it, that's how. Pay the demanded price, at that."

At first they all stared at Dan'l as if he'd just voted for incest. Then several men protested at once. Again Dan'l quieted them by raising both brawny arms.

"Just answer me this," he said, shading his eyes from the sun as he looked at each man in turn. "Never mind how 'fair' it is. Is your land *worth* a dollar an acre to you?"

After a long silence, Morgan replied for all of them.

"It sure's hell is *now*. You know that. We've proved it up. Cleared it, fenced it, poisoned out the varmints, and planted it."

Dan'l nodded. "That's the way of it. Now answer me this. How many of you have ever paid one red cent for that land?"

The unexpected question evoked dead silence.

"Well, yah, we ain't paid no son of a bitch for it, that's true," Nat finally said. "But what right has Birdwell got to payment, anh? He ain't earned spit, heah?"

"What right? Hell, what right they got to tax us?" Dan'l demanded. "Or to make us join their armies? Or shave our beards? Or to fine us for laughing on a Sunday? In England, any estate owner can force your wife or daughter into his bed even though you pay your rents! What 'right' they got? No goddamn right a'tall. But they do it, just like Satan plagues the Lord— from their very nature!"

"Dan'l's talkin' the straight," Morgan said. "But what's left for us to do?"

"We *pay* for our land, that's what we do," Dan'l replied promptly. "We buy it lock, stock, and barrel. And finally we'll have clear title, not just land warrants that ain't worth a cup of cold bilgewater. We buy it one time, on King's paper with the royal seal. One time, and there's an end on it."

No one had expected Daniel Boone to take this view of things. Yet it made plenty of sense at that. After all, a land warrant was supposed to be a promise to pay—someday. Besides, the Colonial Militia of Virginia could put ten men in the field for every Kaintuck, so a battle would be futile—downright disastrous for the vulnerable families.

"Our land is worth the price, all right," Morgan repeated. "But God's blood, Dan'l! Where do I—we—get the legem pone to pay for it?"

"Where did Beowulf get the guts to stand up and kill Grendel?" Dan'l shot back. "He *begged*

God to kill that dragon for him. And God told Beowulf to be a man first. Told him to stand up on his own two legs first, and *then* God put fire in his arms."

Morgan, Nat, and the rest nodded, squaring their shoulders. *This* was Daniel Boone's greatest strength—the ability to motivate common men to uncommon effort.

"We'll have a settlement meeting tomorrow," Dan'l said. "And all of us, working in the same harness, will cut this furrow. Right now Enis Birdwell's laughing up his sleeve at us. But mark my words, stout lads! We *will* make him swallow back that laugh."

Once again Daniel Boone proved he was as good as his word.

He made it clear from the get-go that this was a *group* fight—each settler in it for his neighbors, too, not just to save his own bacon. All would sink or all would swim. Even so, at first few Kaintucks were sanguine enough to believe they could raise the awesome sum of twenty thousand dollars.

But Dan'l didn't give them time to steep in bitter defeat. Knowing this was a game-rich season, the long hunter quickly organized the fittest young men into hunting teams and sent them out onto the game traces. Deerskins were presently worth about a dollar apiece. But the market was also lively for good fox and muskrat pelts.

The effort, however, didn't stop there. While

Dan'l rallied the stoutest men to action, Becky organized the womenfolk and elders.

"We've all seen how rich the Shakers have become by selling linen goods and brooms to the river markets," she reminded them. "Well, there's also a great demand for fine quilts."

"Aye!" sang out Old Man Jacob, the septuagenarian whose cherry-wood dulcimers were prized as far east as Philadelphia. "And fine musical instruments, too. Why, the pioneers're music-starved!"

"And they require good rigging!" shouted Graham Ahearn, a harness maker.

And so it went. Over the next hectic weeks, Jules Robinson turned out dozens of his highly prized rush-bottom chairs. Etty Bainbridge made her famous fancy pillows, thick with silk stitch and French pleats. Even Hiram Steele, who usually showed less get-up than a gourd, sold an entire forty-acre sorghum crop and called it "extry." He generously donated the profits to the common fund.

Becky and some of the other wives spent long days braiding rugs, which were sold in wholesale lots to passing barge captains. These hungry rivermen, whose barge and flatboat crews passed the settlements almost daily now, gave Becky another profitable idea. Women set up long boards on trestles at the river's edge, selling cakes, cobblers, and meat pies.

Even children pitched in. All day long, the younger girls sat churning, moving the dashers up and down, up and down to bring butter.

Then the boys packed it in kegs of winter ice and it was shipped to Natchez and New Orleans, where the dairy industry languished in subtropical heat.

As for Dan'l, he stayed as busy as a moth in a mitten for the next month. For one thing, he still suspected that War Hawk was hiding somewhere in this area, biding his time—waiting for an opportunity to vent his demonic thirst for revenge. With his family always in mind, Dan'l stayed as close to the settlements as possible, constantly scouting and patrolling their outer boundaries.

When he wasn't in the saddle or searching for sign, Dan'l could be found with a surveyor's chain in hand. Over the years, boundary lines had faded, been forgotten, or fallen into dispute. Dan'l wanted all claims in order when it came time to turn in questionable land warrants for legal titles.

As for War Hawk, day after day passed with no further sign of the cunning renegade. Dan'l knew he could never rest easy about that murderer. The Shawnees were a fox-eared tribe, all right, and none more so than War Hawk.

Nonetheless, as more uneventful days ticked by, Dan'l began to suspect either that he was wrong or War Hawk had left the area by now.

Dan'l didn't want to leave it like that. Things between him and War Hawk had been coming to a head for years. Dan'l didn't want this situation to continue as it was—unsettled, "between dog and wolf," as Squire Boone called murky situations.

The best way to get rid of a boil, Dan'l figured, was to lance it, not just hope it went away on its own.

"Boone ain't just sittin' on his pratt," Big Sandy reported to his boss. "I know it sounds soft-brained, but talk all over Boonesborough is about how they mean to by-God post the pony. Every man jack among 'em 'spects Boone to deliver payment on twenty thousand acres."

Enis Birdwell loosed a fluming snort. "Stuff! They've imbibed one legend too many about Boone is all. All puffed up on his air-pudding. They don't stand a Chinaman's chance of raising that money. They've less than fifteen days now."

"Would it really be such a problem," Big Sandy suggested slyly, "if Boone's rabble *do* raise the amount? It's Boone, you realize, who would deliver it."

Birdwell was busy studying a map of the American Colonies spread out before him on his broad desk. He glanced up at his toady, interested but cautious.

"The Indian, you mean? War Hawk?"

Big Sandy nodded.

"You speak well of him as a fighter. Could he do it? Brace Daniel Boone on the trail and rob him? I despise Boone, but I'm the first to admit he's a formidable foeman."

"Straight goods," Big Sandy agreed. "*I*

wouldn't try to rob him. But if there's a man can do it, I'd wager on War Hawk. If he botches it, so? One more dead savage to green the grass."

"Actually, it'd be perfect," Birdwell said, warming to the new twist this trail had taken. "I'm not linked to any Indians of any tribe. Not only could Boone prove nothing—he'd have little reason to even suspect."

"War Hawk won't set any store by the money," Big Sandy said. "Killing Boone will be his main interest. But he knows we value the gold, and he'll expect some trade goods for it, is all. I'd say about a hundred dollars worth of weapons and such will put that money in our hands."

Birdwell noticed the "our," but wisely said nothing for now.

"Good," he replied. "It's a plan right out of the top drawer! We get rich, and Boone gets killed. And we can clear his mountain rabble out of our new country. Let's do it!"

Chapter Five

By the time well-tassled corn rippled in the breeze, Enis Birdwell's two-month deadline had nearly expired.

Dan'l called another settlement meeting to tote up their total earnings. Incredibly, the hard-working pioneers had raised nearly $19,500. It was Judge Josiah Burns who capped the climax by generously donating the final five hundred dollars—his yearly dividend from a wise investment, years before, in his brother's armaments manufactory back in North Carolina.

"Who *needs* England?" Dan'l bellowed to his fellow Kaintucks. "Even a fool can put on his own clothes better than a wise man can do it for him!"

"Three cheers for the giant who opened the Wilderness Road!" shouted Morgan Trapp. "Three cheers for Dan'l Boone!"

But Dan'l interceded before the cheering could begin.

"No! Three cheers for the Kaintucks! It was all of us got 'er done!"

But when the wild cheering subsided, hard work still remained. America's monetary system was still chaotic, with Spanish, French, British, and American currencies all competing. So the total sum represented a confusion of specie and paper: Spanish bits, Portuguese coins, shillings, and pistareens. The very next day, Dan'l set out on the 150-mile ride to the River Merchants' Exchange House in St. Louis, where he converted everything into gold coins.

"When will thee leave for Virginia?" Becky asked Dan'l on the night of his return from St. Louis.

"Tomorrow," a weary Dan'l replied promptly, picking his light-boned wife up and twirling her gaily around the kitchen. "Time's pressing. Now scrape the gravy skillet, woman! My backbone's rubbing my ribs, I'm *that* starved!"

Becky, infected with Dan'l's joy, laughed with him. But as she poked embers to life in the kitchen stove, she stared at the leather saddle panniers behind the door, stuffed with gold.

"Thee take a care, Dan'l," she warned him in a sudden burst of seriousness. "That's more money than a body could *dream* of. Thee just take a care, Dan'l Boone."

* * *

Dan'l did indeed take a care as he tracked east along the bank of the Cumberland River, bearing toward the Blue Ridge Mountains. He made good time that first day, stopping only to rest and water Rip. Dan'l ate in the saddle, gnawing cold fried grits and ham Becky had put up for him.

The late summer sun had weight as well as heat, and Dan'l found it downright pleasant bearing down on his back and shoulders. He pushed on through the scalloped hills of the rising Cumberland Plateau, passing through lush meadows of timothy and clover and white columbine. So far the trail had been easy, and neither man nor horse was particularly tired.

Nonetheless, the lazy Rip occasionally began "limping" from time to time, trying the game with each leg in turn.

"Try another one, old war horse," Dan'l would suggest each time, and sure enough Rip's limp appeared in another leg.

Despite the easy trail and increasing signs of settlement as he moved farther east, Dan'l remained primed for trouble. His breechloading flintlock protruded from a long saddle boot. A .38-caliber over-and-under pistol was holstered on Dan'l's heavy, oiled gunbelt. And a curved skinning knife was tucked into the knee-length moccasin on his right leg.

Time and again Dan'l stopped and listened carefully. But nothing seemed amiss with the birdcalls and insect hum. By now, though he never took his safety for granted, Dan'l had moved his immediate fear of War Hawk to the back of his mind.

Very soon, he would bitterly regret that mistake.

Since moonlight was generous and Dan'l eager to reach Richmond, the explorer decided to push on even after dark. He rested Rip for an hour with an oat bag on him, then set out again.

After several hours, however, Dan'l noticed a hazy circle forming around the moon—sure sign it would rain hard before morning. Dan'l decided to keep his eyes open for a campsite.

The latest hatch of flies was especially active near the backwater pools of the river, and Dan'l tried to swing wide of these—several times, flies had swarmed him and Rip, forcing them to flee. Dan'l was negotiating his way through a huge sassafras thicket when those pesky flies literally sent deadly trouble hurtling his way.

Dan'l heard the sudden, wild crashing of bushes and undergrowth, heard the savage roars of what could only be a fly-mad brown bear—and the ruckus was heading straight toward him!

Even as the wall of green before him suddenly parted, Dan'l grabbed his flintlock rifle and started to throw the stock up to the hollow of his shoulder.

Unfortunately, the wind shifted just then, and Rip whiffed bear—every horse's mortal enemy.

Silvery-white moonlight was generous, and

Dan'l clearly glimpsed the big, three-hundred-pound animal crashing toward him, enraged by a cloud of flies swarming its shaggy head. But just as Dan'l eased his trigger back, Rip suddenly reared up hard, then bolted.

Dan'l's flintlock bucked uselessly even as the big Kaintuck crashed hard into the thicket. He managed to claw his pistol from its holster and fire as the bear leaped on him. Dan'l's bullet only wounded the already crazed bear, enraging it further.

Dan'l felt white-hot pain rip into his left calf as the bear raked it with its razored claws. He managed to get his pistol pointed at the bear again, and discharged the second barrel. The animal shuddered for a moment, then renewed its frenzied attack.

As deadly as those claws were, Dan'l knew it was even more important to avoid the bear's vise-like jaws. He had once seen a bear crush a freighter's skull like an eggshell.

So Dan'l suffered rake after fiery rake of those claws as he wrestled away from the bear's clicking teeth. Again, again, and yet again the enraged beast slammed Dan'l into the ground, each blow like a mule kick to the skull.

By dint of sheer strength, Dan'l managed to roll momentarily free of the bear's death hug. In a finger snap, Dan'l had his knife out of his moccasin. Knowing it was futile to stab through that thick coat and hide, Dan'l went for the tender skin of the nose, the inside of the bear's mouth, and its eyes.

Despite several deep slices, the bear only increased its mad, roaring fit. Somehow, bleeding and on fire with pain, Dan'l managed to break free and roll desperately to one side.

But even as he struggled to his feet, Dan'l caught sight of a figure standing perhaps ten yards to the right in the ghostly moon-wash, Dan'l's saddle panniers draped over his left shoulder: War Hawk!

The Shawnee's face was suffused with wild triumph as he drew his buffalo-sinew bowstring taut. Dan'l dropped back down even as the string *thwapped*.

The fly-mad bear was about to leap on Dan'l again when War Hawk's arrow, intended for Boone, instead punched hard into the bear's right eye. The powerful osage-wood bow could drive an arrow clean through a buffalo and drop it out the other side. This one drove deep into the bear's brain, finally killing it.

Dan'l picked his pistol up, too pain-rattled to recall it was spent. But God finally took pity on the beleaguered Kaintuck. War Hawk, in his excitement, had not counted shots, and did not realize the short gun was empty. With the Kaintucks' twenty thousand dollars in those panniers, War Hawk fled deep into the forest.

Dan'l, dizzy with exertion and blood loss, tried to stand and whistle for Rip. But suddenly he felt as if he was standing in a canoe on a rough river. Dizziness blurred his vision, and a moment later the ground came up hard to claim him as Dan'l passed out.

During that long, oblivious sleep of exhaustion, Dan'l recognized the soft pattering of rain. Summer rain, a trailsman's inner voice reminded him, for trees in full leaf give rain a fuller, huskier noise.

The rain finally stopped, more time passed unmarked, and Dan'l felt heat on his face—quite pleasant and welcome in this chilly damp bed of his. His eyes finally fluttered open, and Dan'l saw that fingers of early morning sunlight poked through the leaves.

Pain exploded throughout Dan'l's body when, groaning from his soul, he somehow managed to sit up. He saw the dead bear, saw the deep, blood-clotted gashes on his own legs—and then memory came rushing back, and Dan'l groaned again.

War Hawk!

Good heart of God, War Hawk got the land money! Dan'l was noted throughout the Colonies as a man blessed with a serene nature in any circumstances. But at that moment, an abject panic turned his thoughts into frenzied rodents scattering about in his skull.

At least Rip had returned to his master during the night. Dan'l's mouth felt dry and stale, like the last cracker at the bottom of the barrel. He struggled to his feet and drank a little from the bladder-bag tied to his saddlehorn.

Dan'l quickly gained control of his thoughts.

He realized he wouldn't be alive right now if War Hawk had stayed in the area. So obviously the Shawnee had fled. Took the money and ran—just like a white man would do.

He *knew* to take those panniers, Dan'l decided. True, Dan'l had no proof War Hawk knew they contained gold coins. But if he did, that meant white men were in the mix. White men like Big Sandy Lavoy and Enis Birdwell.

Soon enough, Dan'l meant to cut sign on War Hawk. But for now, he had to return to Boonesborough and get his wounds tended to. Worst of all, he also had to tell his fellow Kaintucks he had failed them. Their money was gone, and next to go would be their land.

Chapter Six

"You're telling us it's been *took*?" Old Man Jacob demanded in a stunned voice. "All our money?"

"The whole caboodle," Dan'l confirmed miserably.

A shocked, unreal silence settled over the parade commons. The Boonesborough settlers had expected bad news when Reverend Perkins summoned them with urgent pealings of the church bell. But this! This was a soul-jarring calamity straight out of Scripture—literally leaving a people exiled in the wilderness.

"A lot of money and hard work down the drain, that's what it is!" roared out Morgan Trapp.

"Tossed right down a rat hole, heah?" bellowed Nat Bischoff, his face purpling with rage.

"And us left without a pot to spit in!" Graham Ahearn added.

Dan'l understood their anger and did nothing, at first, to quell the outburst. But he knew that hot-jawing would change nothing. He waited patiently for the first shock of the bad news to settle in. When he'd returned the night before, Becky had bathed his wounds in soft cistern water and wrapped them in linen soaked in gentian. Even so, Dan'l's lacerations throbbed and burned.

"Mayhap that money *is* down a rat hole right now," Dan'l conceded. "But happens I know the rat that's got it! And I mean to run him down. Don't none of you plan on pulling up stakes just yet."

"He-bear talk!" a scornful voice shouted. "That money is smoke behind us!"

"Buried in the woods!" someone else agreed. "And maybe Boone knows the closest tree!"

Dan'l had expected some talk like this. But Josiah Burns, the circuit judge, spoke up.

"I caution every man present," he said sternly, "to keep a civil tongue in his head! We wouldn't even have claims hereabouts if not for Daniel. How many times has he put himself on the line to defend us? Your anger is understandable. But I caution you—so long as the People's Court retains authority in these parts, I will *not* tolerate vicious slanders of those who defend us with their very lives!"

Dan'l had far more friends than enemies in

this crowd. The judge's sobering words brought the hotheads to their senses. But Dan'l almost preferred their anger and hostility to this new look of total despair and defeat.

One by one, or in silent little groups, the settlers began to disperse. Jip Adair and Evan Blackford were waiting when a dejected Dan'l descended from the reviewing stand, favoring his bear-clawed leg.

"Give over fretting, Dan'l," Jip advised. "Now it's time to put paid to it. You cut sign on War Hawk yet?"

Dan'l nodded. "I followed it just long enough to make sure of his direction."

Jip said, "Upcountry of the Misery, anh? No point loitering, is they?"

Jip meant the Missouri River. Dan'l nodded. "None a'tall. I figured to take you along, old roadster. That's the short-grass prairie country. Teton Sioux ranges. War Hawk's got him a private treaty with them, I'm told. You at least can palaver the lingo."

Jip nodded, although he himself had no stake in the looming disaster. He had filed no land claim, settling on an unwanted spit of ground near Dick's River. His hovel held little more than a nail keg for a chair and a cornhusk mattress. Jip figured the less a man owned, the less vulnerable he was to his enemies.

"Now hold on," Evan protested. "You mean you ain't calling out the militia?"

Dan'l opened his mouth to reply, but Jip snorted. "Don't fash yourself, lad. This ain't a skirmish with King George's Regulars! A man don't flush one quail with a hunnert hounds!"

"Jip stinks, but he's right," Dan'l said as the three men set out across the grassy commons.

"Right? Why, that old blunderbuss can't even see to button his suspender loops to his trousers!" Evan objected. " 'Sides that, *he* ain't second in command of the Kentucky Rifles, I am! How'm I spozed to lead men if you always hide me under a bushel, Dan'l? I ain't a-scairt to die."

"Never said you was," Dan'l replied. "You're a credit to your dam. But being ready to die is only the half of it, with the likes of War Hawk. The other half is being able to kill *right now*, mister. In a blink. That's all the chance a man gets 'gainst that Shawnee devil."

Jip was still miffed at being called an old blunderbuss. He hawked up phlegm, spat, then said sarcastically, "Every drumstick of a boy wants to prove he's a man before his time."

"This drumstick ain't got jackstraws to prove," Evan protested. "War Hawk done for my family, old man!"

That reminder settled Jip's Irish. "Aye, you've got cause, tadpole," he admitted. "You've got cause."

Evan turned to Dan'l. "Major Boone, Shawnees killed your son, may he rest in peace. I'm powerful sorry for that. But they butchered out my whole family like a side of meat. Dan'l, ain't *nobody* got more cause than me. Damnit, I'm goin'!"

After a long pause, Dan'l growled, "That's damnit, *sir*!"

Evan grinned and saluted crisply. "Damnit, sir, I'm goin'!"

"Both of you be set to ride out at sunup," Dan'l told his companions. "Full battle rigs and provisioned to eat in the saddle. Bring bandage cloth, bullet molds, pig lead. This has got to be done fast as a finger snap. Birdwell's deadline is up quick. He won't send troops right off, but he won't tarry long, neither. We got two enemies to whip. Old Man Time and War Hawk."

Late into the night, despite his plans to set out before dawn, Dan'l found sleep eluding him.

"Thee's full of humors," Becky comforted him, rising from their feather-bed and lighting a paper taper in the supper coals. She used it to light the lantern hanging from a cross-beam. "Thy blood needs thinning. I'll brew thee a cup of lemon-grass tea."

Dan'l nodded, listening to the steady, rhythmic breathing of the children up in the loft. He took a long, lingering look at the home they had created out of this rugged wilderness.

"We've already paid for this settlement," Dan'l said, rare bitterness creeping into his tone. "Paid for it several times over in blood and sweat and tears. Rebecca, it's God's green earth, not man's! How can puny men sit on their duffs in London and deed it off?"

"It does give the heart a jump," Becky agreed

miserably. "And no man has paid more times over than thee, Dan'l Boone."

Even before the birds began to celebrate sunup, Dan'l was up and quietly rustling about. As was his habit, he said his silent good-byes while his family slept on in the ruddy lamplight. He kissed Becky, smiling at the way her night cap was neatly tied under her chin. Then Dan'l climbed silently into the loft and bade good-bye to Israel, Daniel Morgan, and little Jemima.

Then, his jaw set solid in determination, Dan'l Boone rode out to save the Kaintucks' homeland.

"Boone's in for a lively chase," Big Sandy Lavoy informed his superior. "War Hawk is tricky as a redheaded woman."

"He'd better be," Birdwell shot back. "He just robbed one of the most dangerous men in the Colonies. You are absolutely sure the savage fled west as instructed?"

Big Sandy nodded, and pushed his large frame out of the wing-back chair in front of Birdwell's desk. He crossed to the map behind Birdwell.

"I made it crystal clear there's to be no connection between you and War Hawk," Big Sandy explained. "War Hawk will flee into the northwest country. He's got Indian friends up that way."

Big Sandy traced a route on the map while Birdwell savored snuff in his upper lip.

"He'll run upriver on the Colbert"—Lavoy

used the old French name for the Mississippi River—"to the Missouri at St. Louis settlement. From there, he rides up the Missouri to the confluence with the Platte River. That's where I'll meet him and swap a packhorse loaded with trade goods for the money."

"How long will you need to ride out there?"

"I figure at least two weeks," Lavoy replied. "It's about a thousand miles, mostly good riding."

"Well worth the trouble for that amount," Birdwell reminded him. "And don't waste any opportunities to kill Boone once you and War Hawk have him in hostile Sioux territory."

Big Sandy flashed a mouthful of teeth like crooked yellow gravestones. "Not to worry, milord. Boone may be aimed west, but he's headed straight to Hell."

Chapter Seven

"I know War Hawk," Dan'l warned both of his companions. "With him, you can't tell when the chase will turn about into the hunt—and *us* the game."

The men rode three abreast at a wide stretch in the trail. This was their fourth day of hard riding since leaving Boonesborough—their first day west of the Mississippi. By now the two older men's faces were beard-smudged, and all three faces were wind-rawed from constant exposure.

"War Hawk," Dan'l resumed, "likes to turn and attack. He's also partial to the classic ambush from the flanks, so keep your eyes to the sides, too."

Following his own advice, Dan'l kept constant track of the flocks of wood thrushes and jays, the swooping flights of blue-wing teals. Likewise, he kept his hearing attuned to any unexplained changes in the insect hum.

This day, like those preceding it, was brittle with hot sunlight. The country of clear, sand-bottom creeks and unbroken trees was behind them. Soon, Dan'l knew from experience, they would be slapping at buffalo gnats and watching dusty coyotes slink away through jagged seams and gullies—all beneath a sky so blue and bottomless it roared inside a man's skull.

Old Jip had been roweling Evan ever since the Kaintucks rode out. Now the sly old Indian trader saw the youth glancing nervously around them in this unfamiliar terrain. Jip knew that youths back in the settlements grew up hearing monster stories set in the "Great American Desert." The old man began singing, over and over in a gravelly monotone:

Thirty miles to water,
Twenty miles to wood,
Ten miles to Hell,
Evan's gone there for good!

Soon enough, Jip's singing had the lad as jittery as a horse before a storm.

"Your tongue's swinging loose, old campaigner," the kid advised Jip. "Best tighten it up."

Dan'l watched Jip grin and gnaw off a corner of plug. When he had it watering good, he said,

"S'matter, tad? Worried about losin' your top-knot?"

"Caulk up, you old fool!"

Dan'l ignored both of them as he reined in his ginger and swung down from the saddle to crouch over a fresh hoofprint made by an un-shod horse. Just how fresh Dan'l now determined by crumbling the dirt inside the print. He looked at his fingers, then wiped them on his buckskin trousers.

"Still damp," he announced. "Wa'n't made but a day ago, tops."

Jip scratched at the beggar-lice that shared his clothes with him most of the year.

"Happens the Hawk *has* throwed in with Birdwell and Lavoy like you say," Jip said, "ain't that buck pointing his stick the wrong way? You still figger War Hawk has the money with him?"

Dan'l nodded. "It's a queer notion, I'll grant. But look how deep the back prints are. That gold's heavy on a light mustang pony. War Hawk's got the panniers tied well behind him, Indian style."

Before mounting again, Dan'l grabbed Evan's saddle fender and pushed the rig to one side.

"Tarnal hell, boy!" he snapped, for sloppy care of horses rated high in Boone's bad books. "I *thought* your horse was frettin'. Lookit how you're givin' him a saddle gall, you young jack-ass! Loosen your cinch."

The horsebackers resumed the hard chase, pounding their steeds across the river flats northwest of St. Louis—the last frontier outpost of white men. The serpentine loops of the Mississippi had faded from sight behind them as they tracked upriver along the wide Missouri.

Now and then Dan'l halted them while he took to the highest point of land and got his bearings. Boone also kept a weather eye out for the slightest signs of smoke or reflection or movement. Dan'l knew from grim experience that nothing could be ignored safely on the frontier.

Once, when Evan started to remove his shirt in the furnace heat, Dan'l warned him, "You'll catch colic, boy."

"Colic?" Evan scoffed. "Out here?"

"Ahuh. Lead colic. White skin reflects light like a mirror."

Jip, meantime, continued to bamfoozle the boy at every opportunity. At one point, during a break to spell their mounts, Dan'l heard Evan imploring Jip, "*Would* you sell it to me, Jip? Or maybe swap for it? I'll give you my new steel-case knife for it!"

Dan'l, stifling a grin, watched the sly Irishman scratch his chin as if in deep debate with himself.

"Wal," Jip finally said, "you're young. You'll have more enjoyment of it, I reckon. You bargain hard, colt. But you talked me into it."

Jip handed Evan something, and the excited kid approached Dan'l. "*Look*, Dan'l!"

Biting his lip hard, Dan'l stared at the little piece of shiny brown wood in Evan's hand. It was stamped "HOLY LAND." Dan'l himself had purchased one in New Orleans when he was only seventeen. Now it was Evan's turn.

"It's a hunk of wood right off Our Lord's very cross!" Evan said reverently. "A body can see plain where it's even been numbered. Piece number eighty-seven."

"Treasure it, boy," Dan'l said tersely, feigning a cough to disguise his sudden laughter. Realizing Dan'l's plight, Jip was forced to bite his own lip to smother his own laugh.

The three Kaintucks took no time to hunt or fish, subsisting on jerked meat and dried fruit. They grained their horses in quick but nourishing feeds from burlap sacks of corn and oats tied to their saddles. During their four-hour camps after dark, they built fires in deep pits and molded extra bullets while they tried to ignore their growling bellies.

"Your Becky sure-God sets out good grub," Jip announced wistfully at one point.

Dan'l, anticipating sun glare ahead on the open plains, was busy smoking his rifle sights to cut reflection.

"I thankee for that reminder," he shot back sarcastically.

Early next morning, Jip loosed a shout from his position up ahead on point. Dan'l and Evan clucked to their mounts and joined the old-timer atop a little wind-scrubbed knoll.

Jip pointed ahead, into the shadowy lee of the knoll.

"God's blood!" Dan'l swore softly.

A sharpened stake had been thrust into the

buffalo-grass sod. A scalp had been tied atop the stake—a blond scalp, obviously female. And Dan'l recognized, at the same moment Evan did, the distinctive French braid that could only have belonged to Tilly Blackford, Evan's mother.

"Jip, you consarn fool!" Dan'l muttered. "Lettin' the boy see that!"

Dan'l quickly removed the scalp, his own scalp tightening at the touch of it. Evan had not yet moved. He sat his saddle, staring at the stake with glazed eyes.

Dan'l, like Jip, carefully scrutinized the rolling vastness around them.

"That's War Hawk, all right," Dan'l said finally. "Mad-dog mean and crazy. Tryin' to unstring our nerves. Wants to break our concentration, make us careless. That means there's trouble just ahead."

Now Dan'l looked directly at Evan. "That means we got to *forget* this, y'unnerstan'? You got to put it away from your mind, boy, or you're gone beaver."

But Evan hadn't heard a word. He continued to sit as still as a pillar of salt, staring with glassy eyes at the stake in the sod.

Dan'l cursed, and suddenly slapped the boy hard.

"Nerve up, damnit!" the frontiersman growled. "You *made* us take you along! Now, by God, you'll be a man, or you'll point your bridle back east right now! Which is it, *Lieutenant* Blackford?"

The imprint of Dan'l's hand slowly burned a

red mark on Evan's cheek. But the blow had knocked him back into sound fettle. He nodded and shortened his reins.

"We're burning daylight, sir," Evan replied as he spurred his horse forward.

"By God," Jip told Dan'l before they caught up to Evan, "I'm giving that sassy young buck his knife back!"

Big Sandy Lavoy, too, was dusting his hocks toward the west to rendezvous with War Hawk. But he deliberately kept to a trail well north of Boone's little group.

From Richmond, Big Sandy followed the Old Colonial Pike to Charlestown. Then he passed north of Lou'ville, in the new Kentucky County, and on into the vast Illinois Territory. That was the end of any established roads.

From there to the Missouri River, Big Sandy stuck to ancient Indian traces he knew from his years as a special courier for the French Fur Company, once based on Lake Superior.

But along the way, and before he crossed the Mississippi, Big Sandy spread the "news" at every settlement: "Friends, have you heard the word? T'rrific sensation! Daniel Boone has stolen twenty thousand dollars and lit out west! My hand to God it's true! Any man who manages to plug him won't ever have to eat hominy again!"

"We're closing in on him," Dan'l said after breaking open and carefully inspecting droppings left by War Hawk's pony. "Hot as the sun is, this dung ain't even dried out yet."

"Be a damn good thing," Jip observed, "if we *could* catch him up quick. We're already edging into Teton Sioux ranges. The further north we go from here, chappies, the deeper we head into a heap o' misery."

Dan'l nodded, his penetrating gaze scanning the rolling grassland around them. "The Sioux ain't no boys to trifle with. Most especial when War Hawk has made common cause with 'em."

The trace looped back close to the river and led into a stretch of pine tree country.

"Look lively," Dan'l warned his companions as he urged Rip forward to take the point. "Ambush country. Check your loads, make sure your powder ain't clumped."

And perhaps because he was looking for a strike from their distant flanks, Dan'l became a mite too complacent about the trail immediately before them. The carpeting of pine needles had grown even thicker, completely covering the sod.

Rip, moving forward at a steady trot, planted his left forefoot, then suddenly pitched hard toward the ground. Dan'l's very first thought was that the animal had stepped into a gopher hole.

But this "hole," Dan'l quickly realized when *both* Rip's forelegs were swallowed up, was a man-made pitfall trap! The pine-needle-covered framework of boughs collapsed, and Dan'l pitched forward over his pommel—straight toward three pointed stakes smeared black with deadly poison!

Chapter Eight

One reason Dan'l Boone had cheated death so
often was his hair-trigger reactions at those critical moments when other men tended to freeze
up.

The instant Dan'l crashed into the pitfall,
things started happening ten ways a second.
Rip managed to avoid the stakes, scrambling
out to safety before his hind legs entered the
trap. As for his master—even as Dan'l flew over
the pommel, he managed a deft grab at his long
flintlock and slid it out of its boot.

Dan'l did not have the luxury of planning his
movement—it was pure reflex and athleticism.
In the fraction of a second that he was airborne,
Dan'l somehow got the well-made weapon
pointed out in front of him with both hands on

the walnut stock. The very moment it slammed muzzle-first into the pit, Dan'l literally vaulted over the stakes.

He barely managed to clear the pitfall and crash down safe on the opposite side.

"Well, God kiss me!" Jip swore in rare awe. "I just spotted a Boonebird fly over."

"The hell *is* that, Dan'l?" Evan demanded, staring at the shiny black gunk on the stakes.

Dan'l sat up, slapped the dust from his hat, and shook his head. "It's extracted from plants known only to the Shawnees and the Cherokees. But sure as cats a-fighting, it'll air-choke you quicker 'n you can gobble a biscuit. C'mere, old war horse!" Dan'l added, whistling to Rip.

Evan stared at War Hawk's latest treachery, and his youthful face colored up with anger.

"What makes a man so hellish mean?" he demanded.

"The white man's cork floats one way," Dan'l replied, "the red man's another. They ain't meant to get on together."

"Aye," Jip chimed in while Dan'l checked his cinches and latigos. "War Hawk's *always* been on the scrap, and there's an end on it. He's wearin' the no-good label, is all. It's no point wondering *why* that red devil does anything. Just know that he's dangersome. Plenty dangersome."

"Don't fret," Dan'l said. "He's paring the cheese mighty close to the rind now—we're almost close enough to spit on him. He'll tip his hand."

"Ahuh," Jip said, glancing nervously around them. "After he leads us all over Robin Hood's barn first."

"Don't fret," Dan'l repeated calmly as he grabbed leather and swung up into the saddle again. "I been keeping cases."

Dan'l clucked at Rip. "If His Mulishness does not object, would he *move* his stubborn ass?"

The trio of Kaintucks had barely started again when they spotted old signs of civilization: wooden racks that had been erected by Indians to smoke fish.

"Cheyenne?" Dan'l asked Jip, for the southern branch of that tribe camped south of the Platte.

Jip shook his head. "Your Cheyenne won't eat fish. It's Lakotas. We best hark to the signs now."

"Lakota? Thought you said this was Sioux country," Evan reminded him.

"It's all one, tadpole. Their enemies call them Sioux. It's an insult, means snake in the grass, somesuch. Anyhow, *they* call themselves the Lakota, and you'll also hear Dakota. Either will do, but *don't* never call 'em Sioux to their faces."

Dan'l kept an ear tuned to Jip, for the old explorer knew gee from haw when it came to the great horse tribes beyond the 100th meridian. But most of Dan'l's attention was focused on the low hills and ravines surrounding them, unfolding toward the far horizon in brown waves. From long habit, Dan'l made sure all three riders avoided the skyline when they crossed ridges and low rises.

It wouldn't just be War Hawk, Dan'l reasoned. Big Sandy would be meeting with him to take that gold. It *had* to be that way. Why else would an illiterate Shawnee warrior go straight for gold—worthless to an Indian—and pass up a good horse and weapons?

Dan'l's penetrating eyes met Jip's sly ones.

"The no-good label," Jip repeated. *"That's* what that son-of-a-buck War Hawk's a-wearin'."

The Lakota subchief named White Bear led a band of Teton Lakotas who made their summer camp northwest of the Smoky Hill River. Not long after Daniel Boone escaped death by mere inches in the pitfall, White Bear sat smoking in his lodge with the Shawnee renegade War Hawk.

"Yes, Boone is a great warrior," War Hawk said in clear Teton dialect. "But he and the rest of the Long Knives mean to exterminate the Red Nations!"

White Bear listened carefully, but so far had said little. He respected War Hawk, but didn't trust him. This Shawnee had a mad glint to his obsidian eyes. He was capable of instant brutality with no warning before or regrets after. Such men could be useful—but also dangerous.

"Where are these hair-faces now?" White Bear asked.

"Only one sleep's ride south from this place. I left a trap to slow them. Perhaps even kill one of them."

"These *wasichus,*" White Bear said, meaning

the whiteskins. "I have never met any but the nose-talking Frenchmen—a dirty but friendly lot. These others, those like Boone? Very few have come west of the Great Waters. But each time they come, more of my people die from the yellow vomit and the red-speckled cough. They are death-bringers."

War Hawk nodded enthusiastically. The eagle-bone whistle thrust into his topknot gleamed a bleached-white color in the light from the firepit.

"And Sheltowee," War Hawk said, "is the greatest death-bringer of them all. I *will* fasten his scalp to my coup stick."

"Clearly you are keen to send him under," White Bear said carefully. "Perhaps you have other reasons besides loyalty to the Indian?"

"Perhaps," War Hawk conceded reluctantly. "But so have you now—you heard my offer."

They smoked in silence for a few more minutes. Pure tobacco was scarce this far west, and thus highly prized. The Lakota women had learned how to mix it with the dried inner bark of the red willow to make it last. It produced a sweet, fragrant smoke.

White Bear was older than War Hawk—late in his warrior prime rather than just entering the middle. Most of his left ear was missing, chewed off by a Crow warrior during a pony raid up north.

"So if my braves can capture this fearsome Sheltowee," White Bear finally said, "you will give me firesticks?"

"Many of them," War Hawk promised. "Good ones made in the land of the beef-eaters," he added, meaning English trade rifles. "With powder and ball. Now Uncle Pte, the buffalo, cannot escape on rainy days."

War Hawk was referring to the fact that animal-tendon bowstrings stretched when wet, ruining them for hunts in the rain.

White Bear nodded. "I have seen the barking sticks kill. They are big medicine. A man only points, and they kill."

Hearing this, War Hawk realized the Lakota knew nothing about the subtle art of aiming and marksmanship. Western Indians had seen few guns yet. They believed that big magic—not a deadly aim—guided the bullets. But War Hawk said nothing to challenge the chief's illusions.

"Whatever kills Uncle Pte," War Hawk added slyly, "will also kill the lice-eating Pawnee."

White Bear's inscrutable face showed little reaction. But the Lakota hated no tribe—not the Crows, not even the Utes—the way he despised the Pawnees. War Hawk saw one small line crease White Bear's forehead.

"I will send out my warriors," White Bear finally decided. "We will capture this Sheltowee for you, War Hawk. But I warn you now, and this place hears me: I will not give him to you until those firesticks are handed over *first*. If you have spoken bent words, *I* will kill Boone myself just to deny a liar his pleasure!"

*   *   *

Becky tried to shake off her pensive mood, feeling guilty for succumbing to useless worry.

"La, Rebecca!" she scolded herself. " 'The Lord frowns on those just settin'—idle hands are for Satan's gettin'!' "

Becky had been standing out in front of the cabin for the last few minutes, watching a brilliant sun set through the spidery treetops to the west. As usual, she was thinking of Daniel—and lately, of her oldest son, James, felled by Indians at the Cumberland Gap. Becky was strong and had learned to accept Jimmy's death as part of God's plan. But the hurting place left by his absence stayed tender and deep, and she knew that Daniel felt it, too.

All this made her think of Israel, who was out hunting squirrels with his pa's old fowling piece. *Lord, look after him*, Becky prayed as she went inside to start supper. *And Dan'l, too.*

"Mama?" Jemima called out as soon as Becky entered, carrying a ham from the springhouse Dan'l had built nearby.

"Mm?"

"Will we have a Christmas tree this year?"

Becky looked at the parlor bay window. "Yes," she said firmly. "And we'll drape it with strings of cranberry and popcorn."

"Goody, Mama, goody!" Jemima clapped her hands, delighted at the prospect.

Watching her little girl, Becky had to bite her lip hard. The woman felt as if her entire world—her *children's* entire world—was about to be blasted to pieces.

Yes, times were good right now in the settlements. Tomorrow, her children would wake to a piping-hot breakfast of buckwheat cakes, soda biscuits, and ham gravy—but how much longer now before Enis Birdwell sent it all crashing down around them? And what would Daniel be eating tomorrow? Was he even still alive?

Becky crossed to the stove and banged open one of the lids to check the firebox. A moment later she shrieked in fright—a rock had suddenly torn through the transparent hide covering one of the front windows! The rock had missed Becky by inches and thumped into the wall behind the stove.

Now she heard them: hoofbeats retreating into the woods. Even as Becky crossed to remove the paper wrapped around the rock, she soothed the frightened Jemima. "Shush, honey, shush now, it's all right."

But Becky knew things were far from all right when she opened up that crumpled sheet and read the six-word message of hate written in dark blue India ink: *God hates a thief, Daniel Boone!*

Chapter Nine

The folds of extra flesh on Enis Birdwell's nose wrinkled like tissue when he frowned. And he frowned deeply indeed as he read the letter that had just been delivered by a courier from Kentucky County.

In sum, Septimus Luce had written, *I must vigorously protest your repudiation notice, and challenge your legal authority to carry it out. As the political representative of Kentucky County, Virginia, I must also protest the paltry time period you have allotted for payment. Sixty days is hardly sufficient, particularly in this land of vast distances between settlements.*

Birdwell cursed and threw the letter down on his desk. The revenue officer had no real fear of Luce. Luce was a bookish, nearsighted man with pulpit leanings, the type who weakened his own effectiveness by floundering from notion to notion.

Unfortunately, Luce was also unpredictable, the impetuous type. And recklessness might become a dangerous thing to Birdwell in his ambitious enterprise to seize the territory west of Virginia.

Besides . . . Birdwell was not really eager to order troops out in Governor Hammond's absence. Birdwell would much rather see a "voluntary displacement." As for Daniel Boone, he was well out of the picture now—and quite likely to remain that way forever.

Birdwell made up his mind, and sent for one of his couriers. Then he sat at his desk, wrote a few quick lines on official stationery, and blotted them with sand before applying the wax seal. He had granted the Kaintucks an additional thirty days to either purchase clear title or desert their claims.

That measure bought some time by mollifying Luce a bit. It also made Birdwell appear more reasonable. But in fact it only delayed the inevitable. Boone was out in the Far West, and even if he did survive physically, he would most likely return without that money.

So *let* the "living legend" live on! Enis Birdwell would control more land than any other man in the American Colonies, and Boone would call him master along with all the rest.

* * *

"Well, boy, there's the Platte River," Dan'l announced to Evan. "A mile wide and an inch deep."

"Why, it's all sandbars!" Evan exclaimed. "Way you two carried on, I figured it was some river!"

"She's some," Jip insisted. "Some sez she runs alla way to the Pacific. Happens that so, we'll be sellin' beaver pelts to the Chinee someday."

The trio of riders sat their mounts on a low headland above the river. Dan'l, however, had other things on his mind than a discussion of frontier geography. He swung down from the saddle and began thoroughly searching the ground, moving outward in careful circles.

"Pick up War Hawk's sign yet?" Jip asked.

Dan'l shook his head, still scouring the ground close. "He's taking care to cover his trail now, and the Hawk's good at that. I ain't picked it up again since we lost it back on the fringe grass."

"No dang wonder we lost it," Evan tossed in. "With an entire antelope herd running over it."

Dan'l stood straight again and gazed all around them thoughtfully. This was open country—as open and vast as any Dan'l had ever seen. Hardly the place to expect trouble, for it offered no ambush cover.

But over the years Dan'l had learned how danger always gave the air a certain texture. And Dan'l felt that texture now.

"What's the matter?" Jip demanded, seeing the trouble glint in Dan'l's eyes.

Dan'l, studying the horizon line to the north, idly rubbed his beard scruff, by now grown as tough as boar bristle. It scraped audibly against his callused fingers.

"The matter," Dan'l replied, "is that we're smack in the middle of an open range that happens to be the heart of Teton Sioux country. And I misdoubt them're wind devils I see stirring on the horizon."

Evan's face paled. "Where?"

"Squint, boy, and shade your eyes."

Evan did, following the line of Dan'l's pointing finger.

"It's riders, all right," Evan finally confirmed. "Mebbe they ain't seen us yet."

Jip snorted. "In a pig's eye! It's Sioux warriors, and they're heading for us straight as a plumb line. And each buck has got him a string of remounts for a long chase. Oh, it's gonna get lively *now*, girls! Best break out your holy wood, Evan!"

Dan'l swung up into leather and whirled Rip about. "Don't sit there gawking like a ninny!" he shouted at Evan. "Make tracks, you young fool!"

And soon the hard chase was on in earnest. At first the wide lead held in favor of the white men. Dan'l's dish-faced ginger stretched out his long neck and lengthened his powerful stride, hindquarters sinking deep, muscles flexing like bunched ropes.

All too soon, however, the race began shifting in favor of the pursuers and their fresher remounts.

Dan'l reined in and halted his companions.

"Ain't no help for it," he told them. "We have to spell our mounts." Dan'l slid Patsy Plumb—his name for his flintlock rifle—from her boot.

"You know what to do, Jip," he went on. "Evan, put that damn hunk of wood away and watch us, boy! Do like we do. All that counts now is a deadly aim, so stay frosty, boy."

Evan watched as his older companions each sprawled backward against their cantles and swung one leg up, hooking it around the saddle horn to anchor it. Their rifles thus held steady when they laid the barrels across their thighs.

"Get those reins tight, damnit!" Dan'l snapped when Evan followed suit. "Your horse jerks his head, he'll ruin your aim."

Dan'l squeezed back his trigger. The primer popped, and there was the brief click of Patsy's flintlock mechanism before the main charge ignited in the pan. His bullet flew true—a Sioux's pony went crashing down hard, sending the rider tumbling head-over-heels across the sand.

"*That* kissed the mistress!" Jip exalted when he, too, dropped a charging brave. Evan's first shot flew wild, and Dan'l rebuked the lad for jerking his trigger, thus bucking his muzzle.

Evan soon found his range. All three men worked like well-oiled machinery, firing, breaking loose their rammers to recharge, firing again. But the braves would not be deterred. And by now, they were close enough to return deadly fire with their powerful bows made of green oak, strong, hard wood that could hurl an arrow four hundred yards with deadly force.

"Katy Christ!" Jip swore when a vermilion-dyed arrow fletched with owl feathers tore into his slouch hat, spinning it off his head.

"Well, that just flat does it," Dan'l told his friends. "The Sunday hymns is over! Grab leather, lads!"

But that short respite only made their horses more reluctant to run again. Dan'l quickly realized they were forced to the final, desperate resort: taking up a defensive position, against a numerically superior force, in wide-open terrain.

Again he reined in, this time leaping to the ground. Evan was thoroughly perplexed when Dan'l lay down flat, peering along the ground with one eye.

"What'd you lose, Dan'l?" Evan asked uncertainly.

"Dismount, you damned fool!" Dan'l snapped. "Shut your fish-trap and do what Jip does!"

From long frontier experience, Dan'l knew that no terrain anywhere was ever truly "flat." Even out here on the plains, there were always little knolls and dips you could only see from ground level. And during combat, even the slightest depression could take on great defensive significance at long distances.

Now he spotted it—a slight natural sink only about ten yards out. Jip, meantime, stripped his mount of the saddle, tossing it down to the ground where Dan'l pointed. Next he quickly moved his horse into the sink and hobbled it, front legs *and* rear, with short strips of rawhide. Evan barely managed to step back when Jip forced the horse down prone on the ground by twisting its neck around in a headlock. Once down, the unhappy mount was forced to remain that way—a much smaller target now, and also a protective barrier.

Soon, all three Kaintucks were pressed flat, using their saddles and downed horses as breastworks to fight behind.

"One bullet, one Indian," Dan'l told them grimly, his face blackened by powder. "Now we got to make it so bloody they halt their charge. Then our only chance is to hold them off until dark and slip away."

"Now," Big Sandy said bitterly to War Hawk, "you see why they write books about that god-damn Boone. *Look* at that! You see it, hah? He's just killed his third Sioux. I can tell right now that White Bear is about to call off the attack."

The two men were hidden behind a low ridge dotted with scrub pine. It gave them an excellent view of the hard-fought battle below.

Boone's flintlock spat another puff of smoke. And yet another brave threw both arms toward the sky and flew backward off his mustang. Big Sandy cursed. But War Hawk flashed his solid white teeth in a rare grin.

"Once again," the Shawnee renegade told Big Sandy, "you have failed to grasp truth firmly by the tail. All this . . ."

War Hawk nodded toward the battle scene. Several Indian corpses dotted the green sod.

"All this augurs well. A Sioux will fight for many reasons—or for none at all. But there is no better cause than obtaining blood justice for fallen comrades."

Big Sandy thought about that and cheered up considerably. "Makes sense, all right. Before, White Bear only stood to gain rifles if he killed Boone. *Now* he'll lust for revenge. Speaking of gain . . . when do I see the gold you took from Boone?"

"At the same time," War Hawk replied, "that *I* see your packhorse loaded with trade goods."

Big Sandy nodded. "Fair enough. It's tethered about an hour's ride from here."

"And the gold," War Hawk said, "is even closer."

"No hurry right now," Big Sandy said, watching a group of ten braves suddenly surprise everyone by storming the three Kaintucks en masse—not a typical red man's fighting trick. "Let's just hang on a little bit here. Looks like the great Sheltowee is about to meet his maker."

Chapter Ten

"Good God a-gorry!" Jip hollered, his Irish accent fear-sharpened. "They've sent out the red-sash society. Them's their suicide fighters! They won't halt for Satan *nor* the Wendigo!"

Patsy kicked back into Dan'l's shoulder socket when he fired, the huge one-ounce ball ripping a fist-sized chunk out of a warrior's chest. But the other warriors continued swarming forward, and all three defenders were now holding discharged firearms.

"No!" Dan'l shouted when Jip produced his bone-handled knife. "*I'm* the boy they're after. You and Evan pull foot to the south, hear? Take Rip and my weapons with you. Do what you can for me later, old son. But what*ever* the hell happens, *don't* lose sight of War Hawk and our gold! You hear me, Irish? Keep it out of Lavoy's hands."

"Dan'l—" Jip started to object, but his friend was in no mind to debate these orders. Dan'l Boone was known throughout the Kentucky settlements as a fast runner. The frontiersman showed why now as he tore off on foot, bearing due east.

As Dan'l had predicted and hoped, the warriors were really only intent on capturing the great Sheltowee—no doubt because War Hawk had given them plenty of incentive. As Jip and Evan fled south, leading Dan'l's ginger, the war party ignored them. They veered after Boone instead.

The red-sash warriors, on foot, soon realized they had little chance of overtaking this fleet-footed hair-face. But their mounted brothers pounded past them, bearing down on Boone across the wide-open grass flats.

Dan'l knew he wouldn't escape. But he wanted to give his companions as great a lead as possible—for after *he* was seized, the braves might well change their minds about pursuing the other two *wasichu* intruders.

Dan'l heard horses thumping closer, and glanced back just in time to see a fierce, wild-eyed warrior bearing down on him. From the corner of one eye, Dan'l glimpsed the stone-headed skull-cracker just in time to throw a protective arm out.

His quick reflexes spared his life. Dan'l's brawny forearm diverted the main force of the blow, but the skull-cracker still caught Dan'l a glancing blow to the temple. An orange star-burst exploded behind his eyes, his legs suddenly turned to water, and the last thing Dan'l recalled was green grass hurtling upward to claim him.

Spinning . . . Dan'l felt himself whirling, up and down, up and down, round and round and round at dizzying speed.

Spinning . . . over and over, round and round, and the pain throbbing in his temple felt like a foot-long spike going in an inch at a time.

Spinning . . . and when Dan'l finally forced his eyelids open like warped sashes, he was *still* spinning. Or the world was.

The spinning slowed, stopped, and Dan'l, hanging, realized *he* was the one spinning, not the world. The Sioux had gotten hold of a white man's freight wagon somewhere. Part of an axle, with one big wooden wheel still attached, had been dragged into the midst of the clan circles. And Dan'l was securely lashed to the spokes with strong buffalo-hair ropes.

Worse yet, even now a fire was being kindled beneath him. Gnarled chunks of hot-burning cottonwood limbs were heaped over crumbled-bark kindling.

A liquid fear iced Dan'l veins. But he had been taken prisoner by Indians before, and he knew how they treated any clabber-lipped greenhorn who was stupid enough to show fear.

Shouts rippled through the assembled Indians as their prisoner came sassy again. Dan'l palavered some Lakota, but mostly the Hunkpapa branch of the seven families, not Teton. All he recognized now was the word *wasichu*, white man, spoken over and over with contempt.

A warrior with streaks of silver in his braids, but still vigorous of limb, moved closer and stood before Dan'l. He spoke in a mixture of poor English and sign talk.

"I am called White Bear. I know you, Sheltowee! Indian killer, ah? Back east of river call Big Waters, you *wasichu* devils crazy like dogs in hot moon! Kill Indian man, woman, babes."

Dan'l couldn't move his head more than a few inches either way, but he had a good view of the Sioux camp. It had been established in the lee of a long ridge, so it was wind-sheltered yet commanded a good view of the surrounding plains. The day was waning. A gloom had descended over the camp, and Dan'l saw a nascent moon glowing white directly overhead. Big smudge fires billowed thick smoke to drive off the latest hatch of mosquitoes.

"I killed *plenty* Indians," Dan'l admitted boldly, suddenly spitting on the ground at the chief's moccasined feet to show his contempt. "Indians kill plenty whites, too, you bet. They killed Sheltowee's own boy, huh? I killed *plenty* Indians!"

Each word caused a spike of pain in his wounded temple. But Dan'l's defiant actions drew a few murmurs of approval from some of the hard-eyed warriors. *This* was a man, their glances told each other. Dan'l cast his eye about and saw men in leather shirts adorned with beadwork, women in doeskin dresses and bone chokers.

Though impressed by Boone's defiance, no one halted progress on the torture fire being kindled underneath Dan'l.

"No kill you," White Bear said, studying the whiteskin from steady, strong eyes like chips of flint. "Let War Hawk do that. White Bear only test the mighty Sheltowee."

Dan'l knew the chief was sincere enough about this. It was true that, for many tribes, torture of prisoners was a great entertainment spectacle witnessed by the entire tribe and often lasting for days. But torture was also considered an ancient test of manly strength and virtue. How a man bore up to it was the real point. In some cases, prisoners who showed exceptional courage and endurance were not only released—but honored with gifts and great speeches first.

But such times were rare, Dan'l reminded himself as the first flames began licking upward at him. Dan'l looked into all the inscrutable, clay-colored faces watching him, and imagination's loom wove a grim picture of what was in store for him.

His fate, Dan'l realized with a serene acceptance that surprised him, was now in the hands of Jip and Evan—and of course, the Lord Almighty.

Happens I can't survive this time, Lord, he prayed silently, *please look after Becky and the little-uns.*

The flames crept higher and Dan'l winced at the heat starting to sting his legs.

White Bear said something to the brave beside him, who threw more wood onto the fire. Dan'l smelled an odd, acrid stink, then realized his buckskin trousers were starting to smolder!

"Test you," White Bear repeated, still staring at Boone.

"Sheltowee's killed *plenty* Indians!" Dan'l shot back defiantly, even as he felt the skin on his calves blistering in the heat.

Evan and Jip, ignored by the Sioux war party, made a safe retreat to the hard-table growth above the Platte. They quickly tethered Dan'l's ginger in a patch of sheltered graze, also caching his weapons. But Dan'l's urgent order—to keep track of that stolen gold—soon sent them tracking cautiously north again.

Along the way, a heated argument broke out.

"It don't consarn *matter* where their main camp is," Jip insisted over and over, made snappish from exhaustion. "At least pre*tend* you got more brains than a rabbit. You don't try to rescue a prisoner from an Indian camp without an army behind you."

"We just let him *die*?" Evan protested.

" 'Let' a cat's tail! It ain't up to us. Boone's been took twice by hostile tribes, and he ain't dead yet. Boy, it's no point in beating our gums over it. Dan'l is on his own now. We got our orders—and I mean to carry 'em out."

"But—"

"Pitch it to Hell, boy!"

A flash of light, ignited by the setting sun, caught Jip's eye off to the northwest. He stared at the scalloped silhouette of some low hills, his old eyes slitted against the sun. A good rendezvous point, he told himself.

"C'mon, sprout," Jip said, veering left across the grassy flat. "I got me a gut-hunch."

The sun was finally sinking in a scarlet blaze when the two Kaintucks rounded the shoulder of the first hill.

"Well, now," Jip said in a whisper as he reined in. "Ain't *this* providential?"

Ahead, in a teacup-shaped hollow among the hills, stood War Hawk and Big Sandy Lavoy. War Hawk was about to hand over the panniers stolen from Dan'l. Lavoy held the lead line of a heavily laden packhorse.

"Break out your long gun, boy," Jip said in a hoarse whisper. "Now we'll put the quietus on them sons-a-bitches. You take Lavoy."

However, fortune was not with them. Jip had carefully kept them downwind from War Hawk's mustang, knowing Indian ponies were trained to hate the white-man smell.

But wind direction shifted constantly on the open plains, and Jip felt it suddenly do so now. War Hawk's pony immediately whiffed them and started fighting its hobbles.

Jip cursed, still trying to get a bead on the

Hawk even as the Shawnee renegade whirled and loosed a tomahawk at him. It twirled end-over-end, and would have caved in half of his skull if Jip hadn't dropped flat to the ground at the very last moment.

And within seconds, the opportunity was squandered. By the time the Kaintucks could get off a round, War Hawk had scattered one way, Lavoy another, leading his packhorse.

Jip loosed a string of colorful curses.

"Well," he concluded, calming down a bit, "leastways Lavoy ain't got that gold yet. But *we* ain't got it neither, and worser yet, Dan'l's got one long, dark trail ahead of him."

Chapter Eleven

Round and round Dan'l turned on the big wagon wheel, slowly and steadily, first his head, then his feet passing through the increasing heat of the flames beneath him.

Already heat blisters were appearing on his soles, and Dan'l could smell the sharp stench of his hair starting to singe. White Bear folded his arms, and the brave turning the wheel stopped.

"Sheltowee kill *many* braves," White Bear said sternly. "My braves!"

Boone, his face sweating profusely, spat again. "Braves? Pah! Women! I should let your squaws kill me? Let them put the shawl on me so *you* will not be shamed?"

A Lakota who had worked for British trappers knew some English and translated this.

Dan'l knew the brave must be butchering it all to hell. Nonetheless, when he finished speaking, a few braves showed new approval for this *was-ichu's* iron courage and straight talk.

Now White Bear turned and spoke to his people in Lakota. Dan'l could guess the general brunt of his lamentation, having heard many versions of it back east. The chief painted an idyllic version of life before the White Curse arrived.

"Lakota children, have ears for your earth father! A great many snows past, there were no intruders here in the Pahasapa, our sacred homeland. Once, the Day Maker smiled upon his red children. We lived in peace. Uncle Moon was the only watch we kept upon our slumbers! There was plenty in every lodge, and laughter was as steady as the scolding of jays. And smiles like little birds lit upon the lips of our children."

He ain't saying sic 'em. Dan'l thought about all the wars and thieving and hatred among the tribes, all well in place before the outsiders arrived to destroy the "innocent."

Now Chief White Bear paused and nodded to the brave beside him, who obediently stoked the torture fire. Dan'l felt the heat building beneath him.

"But now?" White Bear resumed, pointing dramatically towards the east. "Over the water where the King lives, they are land-starved. Soon the glad tales will be silent in our lodges! How many tribes have already fled west, robbed even of their very manhood by the hair-face

90

devils? And those same white devils come right behind the routed Indian, driving the red man like herds of cattle!"

Several braves shouted their anger. The Indians, too, Dan'l reminded himself grimly, had their effective stump screamers. This chief ought to enter politics, the sanctimonious son of a buck.

But more immediate concerns kept Dan'l from holding that thought. The young warrior tending the fire squatted and removed a knife from his beaded sheath. He held the stone blade in the flames until it glowed with heat.

Despite his resolve, Dan'l cried out briefly when the brave suddenly pressed the glowing blade to the prisoner's exposed stomach. The stench of seared flesh made Dan'l almost retch.

But the long hunter knew this was an important moment in his "test." Somehow, he sucked in the pain and burst into contemptuous laughter.

"Is that all you got, John?" he demanded. "Why, you're a papoose wearing coup feathers, ain'tcher?"

No one needed to translate the fearless contempt in the white captive's tone. A few more braves laughed—a sign of admiration for Boone that troubled White Bear. It jeopardized his authority, which was based on the will of the tribe, not absolute decree. And no chief who played the fool for a white man could hope to lead.

White Bear spoke briefly, and several more

braves stepped forward quickly. Dan'l was untied from the wheel and moved to the grass nearby, where he was staked out spread-eagle on his back. The cool grass soothed his skin, but Dan'l knew what was coming even before the braves rolled a few fist-sized rocks into the flames.

"Mighty Sheltowee!" White Bear said in his bad English. "Roar like he-bear, ah? Maybe better kill Sheltowee, ah?"

"You won't kill me," Dan'l scoffed despite the huge, aching welt already forming where he'd just been burned. "War Hawk runs you, big chief braggart. I'm *his* prize, and you got your orders to be a good dog."

By now the rocks were glowing the color of stirred-up embers. One of the braves, using two sticks, pulled one from the flames. It was so hot the sticks caught fire as the warrior carried the rock over to Dan'l.

"Roar, he-bear!" the chief called out, nodding the signal. The warrior set the glowing rock on Dan'l's chest with a noise like thin ice cracking. Boone *did* roar, as flesh shriveled and the cooking-meat smell stained the air.

The pain was so intense that Dan'l's arching body actually pulled two of the deeply buried stakes halfway out of the ground. Almost immediately, a second, searing rock was dropped on Dan'l's abdomen, and this time the big Kaintuck blacked out briefly under a welling of unbearable pain.

When Dan'l revived, his torso felt as if it had

been peeled open and salted. The rocks were gone now, but Dan'l saw them heating up again in the fire.

"Beg, Sheltowee," White Bear goaded him. "Beg, for we Lakota will sometimes take pity on children and women."

Dan'l wasn't sure he could survive another sizzling rock. But by now the Lakota braves were watching him expectantly. Knowing someone would translate, Dan'l replied defiantly in English, through teeth clenched against pain:

"Who would know more about begging for mercy than a brave whose mother mates with Comanches?"

This insult struck deep, for the Comanche Indians to the south were presently among the Lakota's worst enemies. A few braves snickered outright at the pure audacity of this—such defiance from a condemned man! *This* was the courage that inspired the strong-heart songs sung before battles.

Even White Bear was far less insulted than impressed by Dan'l's fighting spirit under such conditions. But not impressed enough to halt the torture. As a brave again pulled a glowing rock from the flames, Dan'l called on the Lord to guide him through what lay ahead.

Rebecca Boone led her gentle little six-year-old mare to the upping-block Dan'l had placed in front of the cabin so women and children could mount when help wasn't to be had.

She spoke gently to the mare, stepped up into the ladies' side-saddle, then tugged briefly on the right rein, heading toward their little springhouse. Dan'l had built it over a cool bubbling brook about a quarter mile from the cabin.

Along the way, Becky passed Sarah Bischoff and a few other women, on their way to draw water from the common pump. At one time, Rebecca had been the hub of domestic activity in Boonesborough. Now she was a pariah—not one of the women looked up to meet her eye or acknowledge her cheerful greeting.

After all Dan'l's done for these people, Becky thought angrily, fighting back tears of resentment. Now the entire Boone family were outcasts. Becky knew the hushed rumors going about the settlement: how Dan'l, supposedly out to find the "stolen" gold, was in fact hurrying into New Spain to invest his ill-gotten gains in Spanish-held lands.

Becky reached the springhouse, which was really more like a giant cabinet of oak built over the water, too strong for any predators to enter. She slid down from the saddle and wrapped the reins around a nearby branch. Then Becky knocked loose the whittled peg that secured the door of the springhouse.

"Good heart of God!"

Becky gaped, astonishment chiseled into her pretty features. It was said, throughout the settlements, that Becky Boone "kept a dainty table." But now, the shocked woman realized as she stared into the empty storage cabinet, there was precious little to put on that table.

Everything had been stolen! Dan'l had recently killed a 160-pound hog, packing the side pork, ham, and shoulders in barrels of lard. All missing! As was a crock of fresh butter, a bushel of apples, even the huge bowl of wine jelly Becky had made to celebrate the day when clear land titles were finally granted to the Kaintucks.

Thieves were unheard of in Boonesborough. No one who needed food would go hungry. Besides, any passerby was welcome to share, so why take it all?

Then Becky spotted the charcoal message scrawled on the inside of the raw plank door: TURN-ABOUT IS FAIR PLAY. YOUR MAN ROBS US, WE ROB YOU!

Heat suddenly invaded Becky's violet eyes, and they trembled with the effort to hold off tears. Not only was Dan'l facing some new, unknown danger in the wilds—trouble was brewing in the one place Dan'l always counted on to be safe, his home.

That thought made Rebecca suddenly worry about the children, and she decided to return right away to the cabin.

"But you told me that's bad water," Evan warned Jip.

"It is," Jip said, worn kneecaps popping loudly as he knelt in the pale moonlight to drink from a little seep spring. "Bad, but not pizen. Mayhap we'll get the drizzles from it, but leastways it's water. Boy, I'm spittin' cotton!"

Ever since breaking up the meeting between War Hawk and Big Sandy Lavoy, Jip and Evan had stuck tight to War Hawk's trail. By now their horses' hips drooped with exhaustion, and the Kaintucks had to coax the trail-worn animals in the voices of patient old friends.

"Don't make no sense," Evan grumbled yet again as they hit leather and resumed the chase. "Us tailin' War Hawk ain't saving Dan'l."

"Harken and heed, sprout! I'm sayin' we can't do nothing in that camp but get ourselfs kilt. But the longer we keep the Hawk from going there, the better Dan'l's chance of escaping. Boone is gone beaver wunst that scurvy-ridden Shawnee shows up."

But Jip also knew that War Hawk was a mite touched and his actions could not be predicted, which made him a dangerous man to pursue. Jip visualized, too, Big Sandy Lavoy's German cap-and-ball pistol, and he cursed.

"Keep an eye peeled for Lavoy, too," he warned Evan. "We ain't got enough troubles, and *that* son of a bitch comes pesticatin' around to make it worser."

"Eventually," Evan pointed out, "War Hawk will manage to double around to that Sioux camp. What happens if we can't kill him, and he gets there before Dan'l can rabbit?"

"Ah, pitch it to hell," Jip said impatiently. "No man lives forever."

Chapter Twelve

Dan'l realized his only hope was to escape from White Bear's camp before War Hawk arrived to kill him. And to do that, he would have to be physically equal to the exertion—which he would *not* be if this grueling torture session did not soon end.

Fortunately, Dan'l's defiant behavior during his "test" had finally earned him some respect from braves who mattered. Just when Boone feared he might not survive the next glowing rock dropped onto him, an old clan headman literally turned his back on the torture spectacle.

One by one, the other warriors in his clan followed suit. By turning their backs instead of leaving, they stated their loyalty to Chief White Bear but also protested his actions.

"I am glad," White Bear told a weary Dan'l, declaring the test over. "You *true* he-bear, Sheltowee."

"Then let me go. You would sell a true he-bear to a murdering Shawnee?"

White Bear's impassive face registered nothing. "White Bear give word."

Dan'l, teeth clenched against the raw, throbbing pain of his burns, only shook his head in disgust. He was left staked in the main camp clearing. But a squaw was ordered to carefully smear Dan'l's burns with a soothing paste of arrowroot and gentian. To Dan'l, it felt as welcome as a spring freshet in the dog days.

The squaw also fed Dan'l a nourishing soup concocted of buffalo brains and rose hips. Between the soothing paste and the food, Dan'l managed to drift in and out of sleep throughout the night.

Just before dawn, the cold touch of a knife blade abruptly woke him.

A young girl of perhaps sixteen or so was crouched over Dan'l's feet, furtively sawing through his ropes. His hands were already free. The girl's face was obscured in the pre-dawn dimness, but Dan'l could see her bone choker gleaming like foxfire.

Pain screaming in his burns, Dan'l sat up and chafed at his arms to restore circulation. The camp was still and silent, night mist still hanging over it. Only a few old grandmothers were up and stirring, waiting to sing the song to the New Sun Rising. Two of them were crouched at the nearby river, already washing clothes.

The girl moved up closer and handed Dan'l the knife. Now he recognized her. She had been watching the torture earlier, tears of pity welling from her eyes. The clan notch on her feather, Dan'l noticed, matched that of the old headman who'd stopped the torture. Perhaps she was his daughter. This knife was not hers—someone had sent her to do this, knowing a girl would not be watched closely. Nor punished if caught.

Dan'l crossed both wrists in front of his heart: sign talk for deep gratitude and respect.

The girl signed back before she turned and slipped away: a fist tapping her shoulder, the sign for bravery. Then she took that same fist and pumped it up and down twice: *Run!*

But Dan'l was in no shape to run even if he had to. It took a real effort of will and muscles just to get to his feet. With pain jolting him at each wobbling step, Dan'l began limping toward the outlying horse herd. He stuck to the shadows, knowing herd sentries would be on duty.

Dan'l paused at a set of meat racks and stole a hunk of raw side meat—he would soon have all the noisy camp dogs to contend with. Dan'l had almost cleared the last structures of camp when trouble reared its head.

A team of hunters was riding out, and they surprised Dan'l just as he drew even with an isolated, hide-covered frame. Dan'l knew Indian camps, and he realized why this shelter sat on its own hummock outside the main camp: It was the Once-a-Month Lodge where menstruating women were banished, by tribal law-ways, during their unclean time.

Dan'l had no time to debate. Either he ducked inside this taboo shelter, or he'd surely be spotted in another few heartbeats.

Even as the riders drew near, Dan'l lifted the elkskin entrance flap and slipped inside. Luckily, the women scattered about inside were all asleep. Dan'l let the hunting party pass, then cautiously slipped back out into the gray-white dawn.

He used bloody gobbets of the stolen meat to coax his way through a snarling ring of camp dogs. Reaching the edge of the pony herd, Dan'l dropped to the ground, hidden from sentries by the tall grass. Cautiously, he swung wide to avoid upsetting a protective mare with her new foal.

The cool dawn wind rippled in waves through the grass. Dan'l raised his head cautiously to check for guards—and suddenly felt his stomach turn to ice when the weight of a huge snake slithered over his legs!

Dan'l froze, knowing he could be a dead man if it was a rattler. His trousers had been singed off below the knees, and Dan'l could feel the dry scales scraping over his bare legs. Seconds later the snake passed close to Dan'l's head, and the

Kaintuck expelled a relieved breath—it was only a large gopher snake.

Casting one last glance all around him, wincing against his pain, Dan'l quickly cut a good buckskin pony out from the herd. The big man grabbed handfuls of mane and, groaning piteously, pulled himself onto the buckskin.

We'll be huggin', War Hawk, Dan'l thought as he squeezed both knees hard to start the mustang forward.

"You sent for me, sir?" said Esther Emmerick in a timid voice.

Enis Birdwell, busy over papers at his desk, glanced up. One of his downstairs maids, still holding the breakfast bell in her hand, stood diffidently in the doorway that led to his private study.

Virginia's revenue officer smiled broadly at his indentured servant.

"Esther! Come in, come in, my dear."

The mobcapped maid did as instructed, her eyes slanting fearfully toward all the official-looking charts and letters on her master's desk.

"Is there a problem with my work, sir?" Esther asked, offering a polite curtsy.

"A problem? Nonsense!" Birdwell tucked some snuff into his lip, chuckling the whole time. "Quite the contrary, actually."

Esther's eyes lit up like fireflies as she watched Birdwell open a little carved chest and count out some piles of silver and copper coins.

"This is your goodwill bonus," he informed

her grandly. "Ten dollars. A little token of my appreciation for your good and faithful service."

"My stars!"

Esther's jaw dropped open in astonishment. *Ten dollars!* Why, that was a small fortune to her. Ten *cents* purchased a full meal at any decent inn.

"Take it, take it," Birdwell urged her when the startled woman hesitated.

"Thank you, sir! May God bless you!"

Esther swept the coins into the voluminous pocket of her apron. It was said that now and then the rich toffs took a freak to be generous. God knows it happened seldom indeed in the Birdwell household! It was rumored that old Enis even robbed church poor boxes. Esther dipped another curtsy, and was about to leave when Birdwell said:

"Esther? Just a mere formality for my tax records. Would you kindly sign this voucher?"

The young woman blushed to her earlobes. "Sir, I have no learning, I canna read nor write."

"No matter, m'love. Simply make your mark there, by your name."

The complicated legal document Birdwell now pushed across his desk was far more than a mere tax voucher. The former barrister had used his superior knowledge of law and legal loopholes to organize a vast land company on paper. Much of present-day Kentucky had been redistributed to Birdwell's dozens of servants and tobacco plantation laborers. These "goodwill bonuses" were in fact nominal payments for right-of-transfer.

Years before, when he was newly arrived in the American Colonies, Birdwell had planned for this day. As part of their indenture agreements, his servants and field laborers had unwittingly agreed to sell "any future land holdings in the new world" to Birdwell for a penny an acre.

Yes, it was all going smoothly enough, so far. But Birdwell knew he was staking everything on a roll of the dice. Even at a penny an acre, this land purchase was expensive. Years of gambling debts had whittled away Birdwell's fortune. This purchase would deplete his ready cash.

Meaning, Birdwell realized, that War Hawk and Big Sandy had *better* come through. Or Birdwell's cake was dough.

"Esther?" Birdwell called as the maid turned to leave.

"Sir?"

Birdwell was already counting out the next "bonus." "Send Helen in from the kitchen, would you please?"

War Hawk's frustration had slowly turned to a determined rage. Once he reached this point, somebody usually died—and died hard.

Now, keeping a watchful eye on his back trail, he finished spitting a fresh-killed rabbit on a sharpened stick. Working quickly, War Hawk pushed his way into the middle of a thick covert just north of the Platte River tableland.

He built a fire and put the meat over it to cook. Then War Hawk backed carefully out of the dense thicket. Being careful to keep his horse on a bare rock spine, he led the animal away.

There was a trail leading *into* the covert, but no sign anyone had left. The cooking smell from that rabbit would linger for hours, enhancing the illusion that War Hawk had taken cover in the covert.

By now War Hawk's pox-scarred face was sunburned almost black from many sleeps of wilderness travail. Because of those two dogged hair-mouths on his trail, War Hawk had been unable to either deliver the gold to Big Sandy *or* get to White Bear's camp.

As for White Bear . . . War Hawk had boasted he would give good rifles for Boone. And he would, though fewer than White Bear expected. But that meant War Hawk first had to get his own trade goods from Big Sandy Lavoy. And no meeting could take place with these two white curs off their leashes!

The young one was green-antlered and little threat. But the old white stag was trail-wise and knew Indians well. Still . . . this false trail should fox the old one. War Hawk estimated the whiteskins would be here soon, before the sun could move the distance of two lodge poles. And if War Hawk knew them well enough, they would never try to jump a Shawnee warrior inside that covert. Instead, they would wait for him to emerge. Wait hours.

And with the white devils thus distracted, War Hawk could get his trade goods from Big Sandy. More important, he could ride north to White Bear's camp and finally kill his tribe's arch-nemesis, Sheltowee.

Chapter Thirteen

Before long, Dan'l realized his situation was even worse than he'd originally feared. This open country, and his increasing inability to move as his burns stiffened and scabbed, left Dan'l feeling as vulnerable and trapped as a bird in a cage.

Most Indians were late sleepers, but soon Sheltowee would be missed at White Bear's camp. Although Dan'l had a lead, he was unable to push the cayuse beyond a lope, for the jarring pain had became unrelenting.

Dan'l already suspected, from the fact that War Hawk never showed up, that Jip and Evan were harassing him. Jip's trail wits were a match for almost any Indian—but then again, War Hawk was not just any Indian. Sooner than later, that wily renegade would baffle any pursuers. Then, Dan'l knew, he would put all his efforts toward killing Sheltowee.

Nor was War Hawk the only immediate ambush threat. True, Dan'l had no hard proof yet that Big Sandy Lavoy was in the mix. But Birdwell had sure as Sam Hill sent someone out west to get that gold. And Big Sandy was a good man for a rotten job.

All these ruminations made Dan'l recall a haunting phrase from one of Lemuel's recent sermons: *Those who are neither damned nor saved.* I got out of that camp, Dan'l realized. But it's a long way home.

The explorer longed for a sup of whiskey to ease his pain and settle the nausea in his belly. But his more immediate problem was the fact that he was crossing a line of high-ground ridges above the Platte.

At first, to avoid the skyline, he had tried to dismount at the summit of each ridge and lead his pony across. But when he did try to walk, he moved slower than a cat with a torn claw.

Dan'l was finally forced to opt for time over discretion, and rode boldly over the ridges. If someone had to spot him, Dan'l prayed it might be Jip and Evan first.

Dan'l relied on the excellent training and instincts of Indian ponies. He especially paid attention to the animal's delicately veined ears, for they were often the first indication of potential trouble.

Boone finally cleared the last ridge above the

wide, shallow course of the Platte River. Suddenly the buckskin's ears flicked forward repeatedly. Dan'l felt the little cayuse stiffen beneath him.

"What's on the spit, boy?" Dan'l asked quietly as his penetrating eyes scanned the surrounding terrain, searching for any movement.

Dan'l didn't like his present position, but couldn't rightly avoid it, either. Ahead, on the long slope leading down to the river valley, was a wall of deep cut-banks—places where spring-flood erosion had dug out dry-land channels. They offered excellent hiding places for anyone interesting in killing without being seen.

As did that clutch of mossy boulders up ahead on the left, capping a low headland Dan'l had to pass. *Caught between the devil and the deep blue sea . . .*

"Which devil is it, boy?" Dan'l asked the nervous little pony. "Big Sandy or War Hawk? White devil or red devil?"

But Dan'l knew it hardly mattered. His only weapon right now was the knife that girl had given him back in White Bear's camp. More to the point: Even if he could avoid their weapons, Dan'l felt too weak to whip a ten-pound cub.

Meaning he would not even try to fight.

"It's a long lane that has no turning," Dan'l told the buckskin quietly. He looked carefully all around him. There *had* to be some way past that Scylla-and-Charybdis trap ahead of him.

* * *

Big Sandy Lavoy, like many men of his day, believed in the medieval notion of the Wheel of Fortune. Once a man's fortune wheel took a downward spin, as Lavoy's had lately, its only other possible direction of movement was *up*.

And now, Big Sandy exulted as he spotted Daniel Boone crossing the backside of a long ridge, the fortune wheel was definitely spinning up again for Big Sandy, down for Boone.

Lavoy gave a close-mouthed smile at this literal "turn" of events. He was out searching for War Hawk, desperate by now to get that gold from the Shawnee. Big Sandy had made up his mind: Birdwell could rot in Hell; *he* was keeping that gold. Big Sandy could ship aboard a three-master at Charlestown and return to England a by-God rich toff, a reg'lar lord.

Instead of War Hawk, however, it was now Boone presenting himself. True, killing the famous explorer was not Big Sandy's main priority. But if he could send Boone under, that took plenty of pressure off Lavoy once he did secure that gold.

Normally, Big Sandy would not try to brace Boone. The man had the fighting instincts and reflexes of a puma. But Boone's downfall was clear now—he was a broken-winged bird, trapped on the ground. However Boone had managed to escape, he had obviously been hurt badly in White Bear's camp. That was why Boone, as wily as any frontiersman, was now crossing those ridges in such a slapdash manner, failing to cover down.

Big Sandy moved his dragoon pistol from half-to full-cock, then checked to make sure the powder hadn't clumped. Then he slapped his horse across its glossy rump, moving out to the southeast. Lavoy had just spotted an excellent ambush point: that clump of moss-speckled boulders about a quarter mile off.

"You think War Hawk's in there?" Evan muttered to Jip.

The Old Irishman, eyes blurry from watching that covert for hours, shook his head as if Evan were enough to vex a saint.

"I might better go ask him," Jip replied sarcastically.

The two men were hunkered down behind a tangled deadfall. Their horses were hobbled well out of sight back down-trail in a stand of jack pine. The smell of meat cooking had finally cleared out, but no one came out even long after the last feathers of smoke had drifted into the sky.

"I've curry-combed the damn ground around us," Jip said yet again. "I see a trail going in, but none coming out. Course, War Hawk is a cute bastard. Mayhap he's fixed us good this time, tadpole."

Evan checked the load in his musket and cautiously stood up. "Dan'l allus says the best way to treat a boil is to lance it. I'm going in there."

"Ease off, junior," Jip growled. "It's time to post the pony, all right. But *I'll* go in."

"Teach your gran'maw to suck eggs, old man!

110

War Hawk done the hurt dance on my people, and I'm gettin' first crack at that devil!"

Old Jip reluctantly nodded. Green or no, the boy had him a point and Jip was caught upon it. It was the kid's obligation to try now, for weal or woe, after what that savage did at Blackford's mill.

"But don't even bother tryin' to sneak through that thicket," Jip admonished. "We'll use a distraction. I'll hie around to the other side and fire into the thicket, rustle around like I'm comin' in from that side. *You* bust in quick from behind him while the Hawk turns to counter my fake attack."

Evan nodded. His Adam's apple bobbed nervously when he swallowed.

"Move fast," Jip urged the lad as the old-timer slipped away to move into position. "You won't have much time. Keep your weapon at a high port to clear the branches."

"Jip! Wait!"

"Talk out, boy."

"Happens War Hawk kills me? You make sure you *do* for him, Jip! Not for my sake, for my family's."

"Shush that now, boy, and worry about livin', not dyin'."

To Evan, sweat pouring in runnels from under his slouch hat, it seemed like half an eternity before Jip's flintlock finally roared, marking the decoy attack. After that, the lad lost all fear as he plowed into the thicket, holding his musket high to clear the brambles and branches.

"Sold, damnit!" Jip cursed less than a minute later. Both men stared at the charred remains of the uneaten rabbit. "Boy, we just tossed away two, three hours guarding a goddamn dead rabbit! We been bamboozled."

But right upon the heels of this humiliating realization came one that was more important.

"Dan'l!" Evan exclaimed. "Jip, War Hawk didn't set all this up to make us feel like fools. He's gone to kill Dan'l!"

Chapter Fourteen

Becky was making lye soap out in the yard when she saw trouble approaching.

"Children!" she called out sharply. "Stay in the house!"

Becky recognized the two tall, slouch-hatted riders as the Labun brothers, Duane and Ansel. By any measure, they were a pair of the biggest malcontents in the settlements. Duane was suspected in several suspicious barn-burnings, and Ansel was a notorious debt-skipper.

"Gentlemen," Becky greeted them, almost choking on the word, as they rode into the yard. "Won't you light down and have some cold buttermilk?"

They stopped only a few feet from where Becky stood over a wooden tub, mixing lye and ash and pig fat to form the yellow cakes of soap. The Labuns were both lanky, rawboned men with greasy hair and clothing. Each man held lead lines. Their eyes prowled the yard.

"Oh, we mean to have us *plenty* of buttermilk," Ansel, the older, replied as he dismounted. "Matter fact, we come to take over your cow and the rest o' your livestock."

Becky couldn't credit her own ears. "I . . . Pardon me?"

Ansel snorted. He had a hard, tight-lipped mouth straight as a seam. "Pardon a cat's tail, why'n'cha? Tell you right damn now, Missy Fine-Haired Becky Boone. Us Labun boys, we hold a grudge till she hollers mama."

By now both men had hobbled their mounts. Becky fell in behind them as they began purposefully strolling toward the little wooden pens Dan'l had built out behind the cabin. The pens held several pigs and a milk cow.

"I must *insist* that you leave this property!" Becky protested. "You have no legal authority to confiscate our property!"

"Well, ain't *she* death to the devil?" Duane asked his brother. "Mayhap we best take some o' the starch outta her corset 'fore we leave."

"This is thievery!" Becky insisted.

"We ain't fresh from the teat," Ansel snarled. "Your man thieved from *us*, so it's all one, innit?"

"Dan'l stole nothing," Becky protested. "And right now he's risking his life to get your money back."

"The devil he is! Your man's a-tryin' to piss down our backs and tell us it's raining! He figures we ain't got the mentality to twig his game. But we mean to put paid to it, Missy Boone, and you can mark that down in your book. This livestock is ourn now!"

"Partial payment," Duane chimed in, "on what Boone stole from us!"

The two brothers were starting to raise the chute on one of the hog pens when the metallic click of a breech mechanism brought them up short.

The Labuns and Becky all turned to stare toward the cabin. Fifteen-year-old Israel stood in the side yard holding Dan'l's old fowling piece.

"My ma said to clear out," Israel said clearly and firmly. "This is our property. I ain't scairt to shoot this, neither."

Both men wore over-and-under pistols. Becky watched them exchange a glance, deciding whether or not to draw.

"I'm warning you," Israel insisted. "You'll have to kill me, and I'll get one of you first."

A long, tense ten seconds or so ticked by, Becky forgetting to breathe.

"Boy," Ansel finally said, letting go of the chute, "either you're soft betwixt your head handles, or you got enough guts to fill a smokehouse."

Duane, staring at the square, solid set of young Israel's jaw, muttered sourly, "By God, he's his sire all over again."

"Yes," Becky said with defiant pride. "He certainly is."

But as the two hardened men were riding out, Ansel reined his horse around and stared at Becky. "Ain't nobody lookin' to kill wimmin 'n' kids on account a what Boone done. But feelings are startin' to run strong agin your man. There's them as figures they's owed. Next time we come out, we won't ride up in broad day and announce it. And next time, if some of you's get hurt, why, it'll be your own fault."

Dan'l carefully studied both potential ambush points, looking for any sign that might favor one over the other. He finally got the clue he needed from watching the birds.

They remained active in the area around those cut-banks up on Dan'l's right. On the other hand, the birds were completely ignoring those moss-draped boulders on Dan'l's left. Why? Moss was home to tasty insects that birds relished.

That deduction naturally lead Dan'l to yet another—namely, that his hidden foe was most likely Big Sandy Lavoy, not War Hawk. War Hawk, like any Indian, would naturally avoid "forting up" in one confined spot, preferring to hide where he could move at will—as in those cut-banks.

Good, Dan'l thought. Now at least he could form a course of action. Dan'l nudged the little buckskin sharply to the east, angling well behind the boulders.

Almost immediately Dan'l found precisely what he needed: a deep but completely dry creek bed that twisted along a serpentine route well behind the ambush point. Because the dry bed was completely grassed over, it would make for quiet riding.

Careful to stay out of sight of the boulders, fighting down pain and nausea, Dan'l urged his stolen mustang down the steep bank.

War Hawk laughed out loud, delighted at what he had just seen.

From his position, between the Platte and a long, low headland, the Shawnee had watched an obviously injured Daniel Boone ease his way down into a creek bed.

So once again the mighty Sheltowee had turned into a shadow and slipped away from his Indian captors. All the better! Now War Hawk could finally achieve a long-delayed blood vengeance against the man who had made a fool of him in front of the entire red nation. And it would not cost War Hawk any of his trade goods to do it.

Making careful note of precisely where Boone had entered the creek bed, War Hawk aimed for a sharp dogleg bend in the dried-up creek's twisting course.

"Christ, that's all I need," Big Sandy Lavoy said to himself.

Anticipating Boone, Lavoy had propped his flintlock's muzzle on cross-sticks to steady his aim. Now he peered cautiously out from his ambush nest in the boulders. He watched the Sioux war party pounding closer from the direction of White Bear's camp.

Obviously, they were looking for the escaped Boone. Problem was, Big Sandy realized, they would surely flush these rocks looking for the escapee. And these savages had a private treaty with War Hawk, but not with Big Sandy. In their present mood, another white prisoner might be just the ticket—they might very well slow-roast his innards for hours as compensation for the paleface who got away.

The Sioux ponies ran strong, their uncut tails streaming out behind them, so long they touched the ground at a standstill. Red human hands painted on the horses' hips symbolized scalps taken by the riders. Big Sandy knew he didn't want to get into a chase with those ponies. His big sorrel was fast. But Plains Indians slit their horses' nostrils to increase their wind.

But Big Sandy dared not retrieve his horse right now—he'd have to show himself to that advancing war party. So the big man retreated backward, keeping the boulders between himself and the Sioux.

Big Sandy thanked his lucky stars when he damn near backed into the dry creek bed. Lavoy was still scrambling down the embankment when, quick as a whip snap, Daniel Boone rode round the nearest turn!

"Christ!" Big Sandy raised his flintlock and fired even as Boone threw something at Lavoy.

The big man saw something glint in the sun, then pain tore open his throat when Boone's knife found its mark.

Lavoy's musket ball tore past Dan'l's ears so close that it buzzed like an angry hornet. The effort of throwing the knife made Dan'l cry out in pain. But his aim was true, and he had the satisfaction of watching Birdwell's favorite toady slide face-first into the grass, gouts of blood spuming from his neck.

Dan'l cursed when he realized Lavoy didn't have the stolen gold with him. Either it was cached somewhere, or Lavoy hadn't yet gotten it from War Hawk.

Dan'l loathed the idea of wearing Big Sandy's clothing. But the man was his size, and Dan'l's own clothing was nothing but charred tatters from his ordeal in camp. He quickly stripped the dead man of his clothing and weapons.

Dan'l worked quickly, his mind occupied with two problems: locating Jip and Evan and locating War Hawk. Only now did Boone notice the sound of riders nearby. He realized he had a third problem: avoiding White Bear's angry warriors.

Dan'l was still outfitting himself with his victim's possessions when the mocking voice of War Hawk abruptly turned Dan'ls blood to ice water. "A *man* would scalp him, too, Sheltowee!"

Dan'l looked up just as War Hawk emerged from a dogleg turn ahead, a flint-tipped arrow aimed dead-center on Dan'l's vitals.

Chapter Fifteen

Dan'l stared at that deadly arrow point, then glanced up into War Hawk's black-agate eyes, now sheening with triumph.

Dan'l pointed at the dead man's balding head. "His scalp is worthless. All hide, no hair. As worthless as you, who could not even kill me when a bear had me."

"I was a fool to trust Brother Bear!" War Hawk laughed, enjoying this moment immensely. How long he had waited to gut-hook Boone! And now there he stood, as helpless as a newborn colt.

"The mighty Sheltowee! Death to the red man! The hair-mouth so powerful that Indians cannot kill him. *His* big medicine turns arrows into sand."

War Hawk spat to show his contempt.

"But now I shall soon give the lie to such fables! And *your* scalp, Boone, is coarse and thick—a manly trophy I will put on display beside your painted skull!"

Dan'l's eyes, during all this boasting, worked as quickly as his brain, desperately searching for clues to a way out. War Hawk still had Dan'l's leather panniers—Dan'l could see them draped over War Hawk's pony, only partially hidden by an old red Hudson's Bay trade blanket. That could only mean, or so Dan'l prayed, that War Hawk had not yet been paid for the swag.

"The chance to kill me," Boone said easily, "will always present itself. I am an easy man to find, even for one as worthless as you. But only think on this, War Hawk. Kill me now, here, and you will *never* see the goods Lavoy brought for you."

It was a huge gamble, and pointless if Dan'l was wrong. But hope sparked to life inside him when War Hawk's eyes showed a moment's confusion.

"*You* have my trade goods?" the Shawnee said doubtfully.

"Who else? How do you think I knew *you* did not have them? This Lavoy, he was a fool. I found them easily. Why do you think he attacked me? Think on it, Lavoy is a cautious man—he would never brace me without strong cause."

All this made far too much sense to War

Hawk. He stayed silent for some time, turning all the facts over with the fingers of his mind to examine every facet. Finally he said:

"Speak your terms, Boone."

"Easy terms. I don't ask for an even trade. I know you won't grant me my freedom even for those goods."

War Hawk nodded, his clay-colored face wary. "As you say."

"So here's my offer. I take you to the goods. Once you have them, you and I will face off in a death-grip. That was your boast last time you slaughtered innocent people in my neck of the woods. Remember? That you would kill me in a death-grip."

Dan'l's challenge was pure bluff. In his present condition, he could not possibly survive a death-grip match. This ancient Indian knife-fight ritual required the two combatants to tie themselves together at the left wrist, ensuring that neither could flee.

But Dan'l had no intention of fighting War Hawk anytime soon—just as he had no idea on earth where those trade goods were cached. With death only a taut bowstring away, time was all Dan'l needed to gain right now.

Again War Hawk maintained his silence, examining every angle of Boone's offer. Indeed, the Shawnee had much to debate here—including the option of climbing up to ground level and signaling that Lakota war party. But alerting them would prove bootless. White Bear, his pride feathers ruffled, would insist on killing

Boone now—Boone's escape had of course low-ered the chief's standing in the eyes of his peo-ple. So War Hawk let them ride on past.

As for the death-grip . . . War Hawk had no peer, red or white, in a blade fight. Not even Boone when he was in good fighting fettle. And right now, with Sheltowee puny from injuries and exhaustion, was no time to balk.

Finally the big Shawnee nodded. "I accept your terms, Boone. But you shamed me before, up in the big-lake country, and for that I was made to wear a shawl! If this talk of the trade goods is just a fox play, I swear by the four di-rections I will make my next tepee ropes from your gut!"

"Boy, this old coon's fires are banked," Jip an-nounced wearily, handing a bladder-bag of tepid water to Evan. "And I'm so consarn hun-gry I could eat Dan'l's jackrabbit stew, other-wise knowed as yallow-dog poison on account it'll kill coyotes."

The two friends, yellow with trail dust and hollow-eyed from lack of sleep, had stopped to rest their mounts near a stretch of pine forest above the Platte. They were searching for any sign of Dan'l. Jip wouldn't state it in words, but he suspected by now that Dan'l was either dead or escaped. Odds favored dead.

Jip had wind-driven sand lodged under his eyelids, and he was in a crosswise mood from the terrible burning and tearing.

"The goldang West," he said. "Where a man

can look farther, and see less of any damn thing but land and sky. And trouble," Jip added.

Evan choked trying to hog water, and Jip stayed the ɔoy's hand. "Gradual on that."

"Think there's any hope for Dan'l?" Evan said.

"I said don't fret about Dan'l. Thaten's slippery as snot on a doorknob."

But in truth Jip found it hard to believe that even Daniel had survived his present scrape. However, only scant moments later, Evan exclaimed: "Lookit!"

Jip followed Evan's pointing finger, then loosed a whistle. The old Irishman abruptly took heart. "Sioux war party! Dan'l give 'em the slip! Fade back into the trees, boy, quick afore they spot us. We want to fight shy o' them heathens when they's greased for battle."

Evan, leading Dan'l's horse Rip, did as ordered. Jip retreated more slowly, for he was scanning the terrain in search of Dan'l.

"Jip!" Evan called out excitedly behind him. "You got to see this!"

The old trader pushed through a wall of pine trees, then loosed a whistle. The trees had revealed a well-hidden meadow of lush grass. A nearby streamlet of clear water chuckled at them. And tethered to a long line in the middle of the hidden clearing, taking off the grass, was a sturdy, seventeen-hand packhorse. The goods it had hauled were now somewhat carelessly heaped beneath an oilcloth that was weighted down with rocks.

Jip gazed all around the meadow. "Handy as

a pocket in a shirt, innit? Lavoy don't mean to leave them goods here long, though. Elsewise he'd a cached them."

Jip cast another, more nervous glance around them. Then he quickly poked through the goods: several British Ferguson guns, nothing fancy but ideal for Indians because of their rugged, simple construction; flasks of black powder; packs filled with shot; bars of pig lead; bullet molds; scarlet strouding; and brightly dyed glass beads that were valued as wampum beads.

"We'll take the whole caboodle with us," Jip decided. "A man has to spend the coin of the realm. And this here realm is Injin country. Rig them goods!"

While Evan carried out this order, old Jip turned to his own horse and raised a stirrup out of the way to tighten the girth.

"Where we going?" Evan demanded as he tossed the multi-pocketed packsaddle onto the big horse and began loading it.

"To find Dan'l, you knothead! Harken and heed. Since them red arabs we seen are riding south, we'll point our bridles north. Dan'l is out there somewheres."

"Ahuh. So is War Hawk," Evan reminded him.

For a long time War Hawk remained silent as the two men rode, keeping a vigilant eye—and a fire-hardened arrow—trained on Boone at every moment. Dan'l, stripped of all weapons, could not attempt an escape—War Hawk had "necked" their ponies together with a short rope.

They gradually left the region of vast, rolling grassland, entering the high-ground country where the Niobrara River met the rising elevation of the Missouri Plateau. Dan'l, who had never blazed through this country before, now acted as if he knew right where they were headed.

Nonetheless, War Hawk inevitably grew suspicious. They had been climbing a long slope for some time, its lower elevations carpeted with blue astors and white Queen Anne's Lace. But as they rode higher, the way was made more treacherous and laborious by rocks and loose shale washed down during spring melts.

War Hawk halted them to stare upward. The shale-littered slope ended in a parapet cliff.

"Why," he demanded, "would any man but a soft-brained fool ride this far to cache goods?"

"Would *you* look up here?" Dan'l demanded. "Recall, child-scalper, that you have already robbed me once."

As Dan'l had hoped, this remark appealed to the braggart in War Hawk, distracting him from his latest suspicions.

"I see how it is," War Hawk goaded. "Now, like a nervous woman, the mighty Sheltowee will climb mountains and move clouds to hide his belongings from War Hawk! I have *frightened* her!"

But soon the Shawnee was forced to silence

as the slope steepened. Now the cautious horses would place no foot down until there was a solid place to bear it. Even so, they slipped more and more frequently.

Dan'l felt tension building like a spring wound tightly inside him. Time was rapidly running out now—he must make his play, and soon. Mentally and physically, he began to gather his strength.

Off to their right, a fast stream crashed down steep staircase ledges, gathering volume as it descended, then breaking up in a final crescendo on the rock heap below. Dan'l watched the white, loud, furious boil almost instantly gentle in a natural sink far below them.

"Tell me a thing," War Hawk demanded. "From here I can see all the way to the base of the cliff above us. Why do I see no packhorse? I have eyes."

"Those eyes can't look into limestone caves from below," Dan'l shot back. "There's a big one up there. The opening is hidden by that traprock shelf above us."

"We will know, in moments now, whether you speak bent words," War Hawk said. "If so, may the white God take pity on you, for *I* will not."

Try as he might, Dan'l could see no subtle way out of this. And he had only a minute or less to try. He had already made sure that War Hawk's flat, buffalo-hide saddle had no stirrups. Now Dan'l was only waiting for the next time War Hawk's pony took a good slip on loose shale.

That moment arrived, and Dan'l made his life-or-death move.

War Hawk's pony began to slide, and the Shawnee was momentarily distracted. Dan'l had to do several things in quick succession, counting on his natural athleticism to overcome his wounds.

Dan'l's powerful left leg swept out to the side, hooking War Hawk and sweeping him off his pony. The arrow *fwipped* from his bow, streaking so close past Dan'l's face that the fletching cut his left cheek. Even as War Hawk crashed to the rocky slope, Dan'l desperately threw off his pony's hair bridle. This also got rid of the lead line attaching him to War Hawk's mount.

With War Hawk only seconds from leaping to his feet, Dan'l had no choice but wild recklessness. He wrenched the buckskin's neck hard right, wheeling the pony around.

But as Dan'l had feared, from watching that water cascade down, it was too steep up here for such a quick movement. The frightened little mustang whinnied pitifully as it lost all footing and began sliding, then rolling down the steep slope.

Dan'l flew hard to the ground, bounced a few times like a tumbling log, then began sliding with his horse, faster and faster, taking shale and rocks with them in a gathering slide that prompted Dan'l to quickly make peace with the Creator.

Chapter Sixteen

Everything was happening fast—far too fast to control any of it. For Dan'l, caught up in the first phase of a massive rock slide, his lifetime had suddenly collapsed down into a few critical seconds.

Dan'l knew there was no way a healthy man could survive this long plummet, let alone a man in his battered condition. Even now, he saw the buckskin just below him, huge and bloody gashes already pocking its flanks.

Dan'l raised one arm for protection as he slammed into a boulder. He bounced off it hard, then felt himself being skinned alive as he skidded through sharp pieces of flint and broken scree.

The noise was terrific, as was the gathering

cloud of dust. Dan'l felt bushes slapping and tearing at him, then suddenly saw a sapling hurtle past.

Dan'l had no time to think, only to react. He flung both powerful arms out, gained a purchase on the sapling, and hung on for dear life as the slope crumbled around him.

"The troops are all quartered now, milord," reported a redcoat sergeant, waiting outside under the open fly of Enis Birdwell's tent.

Birdwell, busy putting the finishing touches on some newly inked deeds, glanced up from his portable "field desk." It was a lidded wooden box that fit across his knees.

"Very good, Sergeant Troy. Any trouble from the local settlers?"

While he asked this question, Birdwell stood up and stepped outside his tent. Coppery late-afternoon sunshine drenched the tent-crowded common square of Boonesborough.

"They're bloody pissed that we're here," Troy confessed in the coarse accent of London's Fleet Street. "But no trouble yet besides insults and dirty looks."

"They hate having troops quartered here. But the truth is, they've had a free hand of it for too long now. With malcontent rebels like Boone stirring them up, they've lost all respect for legitimate authority."

Again Birdwell glanced at his stack of new property deeds. Though it left him penniless, he had finally paid off all of his servants and laborers and drawn up deeds for their supposed holdings in and around Boonesborough. All those deeds were now duly transferred into Birdwell's name—or rather, the name of his new land company, Magna Carta Enterprises ("Land for the common man!").

Granted, the complete success of Birdwell's scheme was far from assured, he realized. Especially if Big Sandy Lavoy failed to return with that twenty thousand dollars in gold. Given the heady events of the 1770's, the impermanence of national loyalties, and the constant clamor of conflicting land claims, a man must also hope for a long ration of good luck. But he was now in a better position than any other claimants—especially considering Birdwell's long history of useful service to the British Monarch.

"How about the local militia?" Birdwell said. "Any threats from them?"

Troy grinned. "Aye, they've held some training o' sorts. But they have no officer to lead them. And they've families right by."

Birdwell nodded, understanding the unspoken suggestion: No one really believed the settlers would endanger their families to fight a hopeless battle against the best Regular Army in the world.

Nonetheless, Birdwell had found it necessary to quarter troops in Boonesborough. The thirty-day extension he'd granted the settlers was not yet expired, true. But Birdwell could not be sure when Governor Hammond might return from London. He wanted these people gone, and new residents working the land, by the time Hammond returned.

Birdwell noticed a group of civilian men gathered on the long east flank of the parade field.

"Keep an eye on that bunch," he warned Sergeant Troy. "They've something tucked up their sleeves."

"They best *leave* it up their sleeves," Troy assured his superior. "If not, it's their funeral."

But the treachery going forward was not planned against the redcoat invaders.

"Why," demanded Ansel Labun to a small circle of listeners, "should Boone have anything left to him? Possessions *or* family? Ain't he as good as kilt our families?"

"And now," his brother Duane tossed in, "that thievin' bastard Boone is puttin' our money to good use for him and his. *That* cock-chafer won't be a-hurtin'!"

"Ain't them soljers' fault, neither," Ansel said, nodding toward the military encampment. "They take orders, is all. It's Boone's thievin' what pushed all this."

Thus it went, back and forth, the two Labun brothers gradually bringing other men around to their view of it. They could never sway a majority hereabouts, for too many of the settlers were of better moral fiber. And they also knew their deep debt to Daniel Boone.

But a majority was never required to cause misery. After more persuasion, about a half-dozen men had nodded in agreement.

"Then it's settled," Ansel announced just before the group dispersed. "There'll be a meetin' first at our place to work out the actual plan. It's got to be did right, fellas. No witnesses, and keep a stopper on your gobs—nary a word to nobody. We'll see how goddamn rich Boone feels after he buries his wife and youngens."

Boone was finally dead.

War Hawk still had trouble believing it. But did he not have eyes to see? He was not drunk, and this was no dream vision placed over his eyes to deceive him. *Boone was dead!*

The Shawnee, having searched in vain for Boone's "limestone cave" above, had made the long, careful slog to the bottom of the slope. He found a massive heap of still-warm rock and scree.

And there it was, protruding from the heap— one hind leg of the crushed buckskin.

Boone was dead! Let the Yellow River run clear, the sun circle the moon! Nothing could have survived that battering, that long, fast fall.

At first War Hawk felt a little sting of disappointment. He had hoped, for so long, to take a more direct hand in Boone's death.

Still . . . War Hawk looked at the big heap, and a little smile gradually ousted his frown. Still . . . it must have been a painful death. Bones smashed, organs ruptured. Elation prickled the back of his neck as War Hawk realized . . . finally it was done. Daniel Boone was dead!

Now, War Hawk realized, there was nothing else for it. The heavy panniers full of the white man's glitter coins were just useless weight to War Hawk. But any fool could see it was of great value indeed to Enis Birdwell.

War Hawk's only choice now was to return east of the Great Waters and parley with Birdwell directly.

Dan'l didn't budge one foot until War Hawk rode off bearing due east. God had worked one miracle already when that sapling held Dan'l's weight; he'd managed to swing himself sideways, out of the main thrust of the slide. And there had been just enough stunted growth to hide him when War Hawk returned below.

Tired, hungry, his burn-scarred torso on fire with throbbing pain, Dan'l made the long descent in the fading sunlight. He knew War Hawk believed him to be dead. Dan'l had also guessed why the Shawnee dusted his hocks eastward. War Hawk didn't know how to spend gold, but he sure-God knew where to take it.

The sun was setting in a huge scarlet blaze of glory by the time Dan'l reached the base of the slope and found the dead pony. He decided to take a chance and build a signal fire for Jip and Evan. War Hawk should be long gone, and by now any Sioux outriders would have returned to camp. It was powerful bad medicine to get caught outside the firelight after dark.

Dan'l crumbled bark for kindling, then heaped big limbs onto the fire. Sawing flames leaped up toward the heavens, shedding sprays of glowing sparks. While he waited, Dan'l killed a hen pheasant with a well-aimed rock. He rough-gutted the bird with a sharp stone, then spitted it and roasted it in the edge of the big signal fire. The meat was greasy and gamey-tasting. But Dan'l welcomed the solid weight in his belly.

Dan'l willed himself vigilant. However, as the long night ticked by, his eyelids grew heavier.

Out beyond the circle of flickering yellow-orange firelight, Dan'l heard a stick snap. He was instantly alert. The big man picked up a stout club he had selected while gathering firewood.

A bit ring clinked, and Dan'l faded back into the shadows. He raised the club, ready to swing it.

"Hallo, the fire!" Jip Adair's thick Irish accent sang out. "Dan'l Boone, you ugly son of trouble! That you?"

Relief washed over Dan'l, and he tossed his club into the snapping flames.

"No, you old fool, it's the consarn Pope! Evan with you?"

"Lieutenant Blackford, present and accounted for, Major Boone! We got Rip and your guns, too."

"Good men!"

Dan'l stepped into the firelight at the same

moment his friends did. "Glad to see you, boys. Big Sandy is dead. But War Hawk ain't. And that son of a buck has took our gold east to Birdwell!"

Chapter Seventeen

Jip treated Dan'l's burns with a foul-smelling but effective poultice of boiled sassafras and moss. Only hours after Jip plastered the mess on him, Dan'l could take a deep breath again without groaning at the pain.

"Watch for dust puffs," Dan'l warned both his friends soon after the trio rode out from the Platte Valley, tracking War Hawk eastward. "Watch your horse's ears, too. White Bear's Lakota ain't likely to just let us pull stakes and leave."

The three Kaintucks rode in single file, following the Perdition River through rolling scrubland claimed by the Spanish but ruled by the Sioux. A lead line tied to Evan's saddle secured Big Sandy Lavoy's packhorse.

"I wunner if Birdwell has run everybody out of Boonesborough by now," Jip declared.

Dan'l, his penetrating gaze constantly in motion, shook his head. "The Lord knows, and He ain't telling. I just pray it ain't come down to lead-peddlin'. Without the general here"—Dan'l nodded toward Evan—"the Kentucky Rifles ain't got a chance."

Evan fired back with his own sarcasm, for the lad had learned to give as much as he took from these two masters. But all of this left Dan'l feeling bitter at his core. Especially when he recalled the triumphant moment when the Kaintucks, against all odds, had raised twenty thousand dollars. Boone also thought about all the human hopes War Hawk and his white cronies had destroyed when they stole that money. Becky's among them.

Dan'l could tell that Evan, too, was thinking of the barbaric crimes of War Hawk. Recalling in particular, no doubt, the horror of seeing his own mother's scalp deliberately planted to taunt him.

"Just put it out of your mind, Evan," Dan'l said calmly. "It ain't easy, but push it on out. War Hawk works on a man the same way Satan does—by planting sick and hellish pictures in your mind to work on it like a canker worm."

"Work on a cat's tail!" old Jip cut in, all in a welter of excitement. "Sioux war party, Dan'l! They been usin' them cottonwoods as a blind."

"I seen 'em five minutes ago, you half-blind old goat," Dan'l said calmly. And indeed, now

his companions saw that Dan'l had already untied the lead line from Evan's saddlehorn. The
big explorer swung down and quickly hobbled
the packhorse foreleg to rear.

"We'll see if you know gee from haw about
Indians," Dan'l told Jip as he swung up into
leather again.

"It'll work, ladies," Jip said smugly. "That's
how's come I took 'em goods. Now with your
Plains Innun? You can ride across their ranges
safe as anything *if* you leave 'em a gift to the
place."

"By God, it better work," Dan'l muttered.
"Must be a score of bucks in that war party, and
look how many mounts on their strings. And us
on beat-out horses in country with nothing to
cover our sitters but sky."

"This old man here is full of bunk," Evan said.
"His brain's gone soft."

"Both you mouth-pieces was on ma's milk
when *this* coon hit the trail," Jip boasted. "It'll
work."

And the old trader proved right yet again. The
war party stopped, examined the tribute, and
simply abandoned their chase. This was more
than a gift from men—such riches came from
the holy ones. Already, several warriors were
dancing their thanks.

"Now, thanks to Jip, we're shut of White
Bear," Dan'l said. "You boys got any more
tricks, break 'em out. We're riding into some
rough weather."

*   *   *

Long before he reached the trace at the Cumberland ridge, War Hawk had learned the news from Indian runners: The white beef-eater chief, Enis Birdwell, had taken soldiers to Boonesborough.

All the better! That was even closer. War Hawk knew some of the local half-breeds who played the dog for whiteskins. He sent one of them to Birdwell with an offer: meet War Hawk at a deserted French fort nearby if Birdwell was interested in the gold.

Not surprising, Birdwell *was* interested. Extremely interested. War Hawk exchanged those glitter coins for a red man's fortune in goods.

"Well," Dan'l finally said, "leastways it ain't got down to a shootin' war yet."

"No," Jip agreed. "But that's gilding the lily, Boone boy. It's about one fox step away from a goldang shootin' war."

"Tory bastards," Evan muttered through clenched teeth. " 'Soldiers' my sweet aunt! King George's vultures is what they are."

"Them soldiers," Dan'l said, "are small potatoes. It's that flesh-nosed bastard Birdwell who's the big bushway here."

The three friends shared a long, wooded ridge overlooking Boonesborough. Below, the common square was teeming with red tunics. Small patrols moved everywhere.

"The hell we going to do?" Evan demanded.

"Nothing, by daylight," Dan'l said. "We stay holed up. Jip might be safe showing himself.

But they'll be looking for me and you, Evan. They don't want the militia to rise up on its hind legs."

Jip looked at his old trail companion. "*Will* it rise up, Major Boone?"

"Does a bear sleep in the woods?" Dan'l nodded toward the occupied settlement below. "This has got long past paying on demand. Now it's a by-God fight to the finish."

"Speaking of paying on demand," Evan said. "You think War Hawk delivered that gold to Birdwell?"

Dan'l nodded. "I'd wager he has be now. And Birdwell is makin' a piker play with that money. Means to take the gold *and* our land."

Dan'l couldn't quite spot his own place from here—it lay just beyond the next brushy hollow. But he knew it was probably under constant surveillance. For now, as much as he missed his family, he must avoid them by day for their own safety.

"Lieutenant Blackford!" Dan'l said abruptly.

"Sir?"

"You'll lay low until sunset. Then you make the rounds of the settlement. Tell every man in the Rifles: We form up at dawn at the gravel ford on Dick's River. Every man in full battle rig. Report back here when you're done."

"Yessir!"

"After dark," Dan'l said, "me 'n' Jip're going to see Becky and find out what she knows." Dan'l took a long, careful look toward the hills behind them. "Redcoats ain't the only problem we got to flush. That bastard War Hawk is out there somewheres, too. Keep your noses to the wind, boys, and watch your topknots."

Huge banks of clouds kept blowing over the moon, throwing the woods in and out of darkness. With their flintlocks at the ready, Dan'l and Jip leapfrogged from tree to tree, moving in closer to Dan'l cabin. Light glowed from within, and Dan'l could see his family moving around inside.

As Boone had guessed, soldiers too were watching the cabin. They had set up two picket outposts, one near the road out front, the other in the trees behind the cabin.

"The bastards are drunk," Jip whispered. "I can whiff sour mash from here. Won't be baby's work to slip past 'em."

Jip was right. Dan'l might well have boldly knocked on his front door without being spotted. But while the two men were making their way around a back corner of the house, Dan'l stopped Jip with a hand on his arm.

"Look yonder," Dan'l whispered. He pointed toward the picket outpost behind the cabin. A group of shadowy figures had slipped past the outpost, a group obviously seen and ignored by the British soldiers. Several of the figures headed for the cabin, others for the pens and outbuildings.

"See that crooked stove-lid hat?" Jip said. "One of 'em is that trouble-seeking son of a bitch Ansel Labun."

Dan'l's well-trained nose sampled the air: *coal oil!*

"Christ Almighty! Jip, they're fixen to torch the place! You bust up that bunch out back. Then hightail it back to camp."

Dan'l couldn't worry now about discretion or British soldiers. With his family's safety on the line, Dan'l *wanted* everyone to know that he was back—and ready to deal misery to any low-crawling bastards who menaced his family.

A shadowy form was still splashing coal oil onto the split logs at the cabin's rear when Dan'l called out boldly, "Hell's got a special room for women-and child-killers, and you're about to move in!"

There was a curse; then the figure dropped the bucket of coal oil and whirled around, clawing an over-and-under pistol from his belt. Dan'l caught a glimpse of Ansel Labun's coarse-grained features. Then the long hunter shot the murdering criminal point-blank, the big lead ball slamming Labun into the cabin with a surprised *"Oomph!"*

In a heartbeat, Dan'l had his own pistol out, snapping off a round at a second figure nearby. Meantime, out back, Jip's flintlock roared and a howl of pain split the night.

"Stay inside, Israel!" Dan'l roared out. And just to serve notice, Boone added in a roaring voice, "This is Dan'l Boone! I'll kill *any* yellow-bellied egg-sucker who lays a hand on my family. That's a vow in God's name!"

Dan'l heard Jip taking off as planned. But

Boone faded back into the trees for a time to make sure his family was safe for the nonce. By now, the surviving intruders had bolted into the trees like dogs with their tails on fire. Nor did any of those soldiers appear ready to play the hero—a few shillings a month hardly motivated a bloke to chase the likes of Dan'l Boone in a dark forest.

That tears it, Dan'l realized as he headed back toward the rendezvous camp on the ridge. They know I'm back. Now it's time to fight or show yellow. Tomorrow was going to be a bloody day.

Chapter Eighteen

Dick's River, where Jip Adair had built his little hovel, was actually a big creek that fed into the Kentucky River. Two miles west of Boonesborough, near the big gravel ford, the Kentucky Rifles formed up for their first battle.

Evan had done his duty, spreading the word all through the night. The men had shown up to the last volunteer. Jip and Dan'l watched them form into squads in the dawn mist, dressed in their butternut-dyed uniforms, muskets and flintlocks held at inspection-arms for the final battle check.

Dan'l ordered sentries out first thing. He had already seen one army—General Braddock's— blasted to pieces while they were still mustering to attack.

"If the Lord was offering choices," Dan'l told his men, "I'd just as lief form us up into small skirmish teams and whip them redcoats Indian-fashion. Draw 'em into the trees and break up their formation. But with so many women and kids scattered hereabout, that's out. We want to draw the troops well away from the settlement first."

"How?" Nat Bischoff demanded. "Invite them to a gott-damned tea party?"

"This is *not* Fiddler's Green, mister!" Evan snapped at Bischoff. "You're in a military formation! Either request permission to speak, or keep your damn mouth shut while our commander is talking!"

Bischoff scowled at the younger man, but drew up at attention and shut his mouth. Dan'l knew Nat as an eternal complainer, but a man who followed orders.

"By God," muttered Jip so only Dan'l could hear, "our pup is a full-growed dog."

"Regroup on the far side of the river," Dan'l ordered. "Every man will charge his piece, but don't ram home a ball yet. We're going to raise a ruckus, is all."

The two platoons filed easily across the gravel bars, barely wetting their boot tops. When they were formed up again, Dan'l ordered all one hundred men to discharge their weapons on his command.

The volley took on incredible volume in the dawn stillness, a cracking explosion like a giant ice floe snapping apart. It echoed forcefully through the woods and hollers, instantly silencing the "dawn chorus" of the birds.

"There! We've told them we're ready for 'em," Dan'l told his men. "I know redcoats—they'll be coming. Evan, make sure they fire another volley a little while after Jip and me leave."

Evan paled a bit, realizing Dan'l was leaving him in command. "Leave? Where you going, Dan—I mean, Major Boone?"

"Don't fret, I'll be back for the battle, happens I'm still sassy. But I got me a God-fear about Birdwell and our gold."

Evan gave that a few seconds, then nodded, understanding. "Now that a battle is shaping up, he might light out with it."

Dan'l nodded as he stepped up into leather and reined his ugly ginger around. "Never mind that damned acting," he growled when Rip commenced to "limping."

Dan'l looked at Evan again. "Post one platoon in a staggered echelon close to the river as a lure. Keep the other in reserve back in the trees. 'Member how we drilled 'em in the two-volley attack?"

Evan swallowed hard, then nodded. "Forward platoon fires, then kneels to reload while the rear platoon steps forward and fires over their heads."

"That's it," Dan'l said. "Redcoats only got one battle style, and they're good at it—advance and fire at the full-front face. They're fair marksmen and they got the numbers on us, so they won't hold back. Evan, stay frosty when the shooting starts."

"The moment that front platoon fires," Jip threw in, "make damn sure they kneel *quick* so's the reserve force don't blow their conks off."

"Jip's right," Dan'l said, nodding. "And make sure they reload the moment they kneel. Happens there's no time to load, fix bayonets or use your weapons as a war club. You got all that?"

"Yessir!"

"Repeat it to me."

Evan did so to Dan'l satisfaction.

"Good," Dan'l told the lad. "Now go over it good with the squad leaders. I'll be back when I can. C'mon, Jip! You was frettin' about your placid, punkin-butter life, anh? So let's go get you killed, old-timer!"

Dan'l and Jip knew every stump and boulder and fox den in the area. Thus, they made it back to the common square without encountering British vedette riders or pickets. The troops had still been sleeping when the volleys were fired at Dick's River. They were still mustering for their offensive as Dan'l and Jip crept up to the final line of silver spruce trees.

"Birdwell's horse is still picketed out front of his tent," Jip observed. "So he ain't left yet. 'Less the bastard snuck out on another horse."

"He's still here," Dan'l guessed. "He'll not want witnesses, so he'll wait for the troopers to leave. I got to get inside that tent."

Jip snorted. "Boone, is your garret furnished?

He's got a hunnert yards of open ground around him and twice that many firesticks within range. They'll shoot Dan'l Boone to rag tatters and sell the tatters!"

"That's the way of it," Dan'l agreed. "But lookit yonder."

Dan'l pointed left, and Jip followed his finger. Near the tree line, perhaps thirty yards away, a young private was standing guard near a "company pile." These were piles of non-essential gear that was left behind, under guard, during battles.

Jip grinned. The pile included a few extra uniforms.

"Nobody'll likely miss the guard for a few seconds," Dan'l told Jip. "But he can't just disappear. How you feel about joining King George's Regulars, old roadster?"

"I'd rather be a turd in the Thames," Jip shot back. "But needs must when that ol' Satan drives! Let's get 'er done, Boone, and damn the cowards!"

The two men slipped closer to the young sentry, staying back in the trees. Jip, unlike Dan'l, was not a known threat to the authorities. He stepped into plain view and called out in a querulous, whining-old-man's voice: "Sonny? What's on the spit, lad?"

Dan'l, still well hidden, watched the soldier start.

"What the—why, God's blood, you batty old fool! You scared bloody 'ell out of me! Get along with you now, or I'll—*oomph!*"

Dan'l struck the moment the private was fully distracted. He reached out from cover, grabbed the soldier by the shoulders, and brutally rammed his head into a tree, knocking him unconscious. Dan'l took no pleasure in the act. But this close to home and hearth, pity was in short supply.

Jip leaped out, snatched a tunic and trousers off the pile, and both men quickly stripped their own clothing and donned uniforms.

"I reckon you'll do from a distance," Dan'l said as Jip stepped back out into the open to take the guard's place. "Just hope nobody comes over here close and notices you're as old as Methuselah."

The tunic was too small for him, but Dan'l managed to squeeze into it, his muscles popping the seams, and get a few of the buttons looped. He threw Patsy onto his shoulder, donned the private's tricorn hat, and strode boldly out into the open, aiming for Birdwell's tent in the center of the clearing.

Dan'l felt curious eyes on him and tried to step smartly along, like a courier running a message. He hoped he was too far away for anyone to notice the ridiculous fit of his uniform. Luckily, the troops were now busy with the final staging preparations before they moved out.

Dan'l ducked under the fly of Birdwell's tent, then pushed boldly inside. The revenue officer, hastily cramming papers into a chamois pouch, looked up with an irritated frown.

"What is it, Private?" he demanded. "If Sergeant Troy sent you, tell him I must forgo inspecting the troops. I'm in a hurry."

Dan'l cast his eye quickly about, but could not immediately spot his saddle panniers. Unless the gold had been transferred to something else . . .

"You're in a hurry, all right. A hurry to steal what ain't yours, Birdwell," Dan'l said, swinging his rifle up to the ready. "But you see, ain't nothing on God's green earth that comes quicker 'n' death. Now, where's that gold?"

The confusion on Birdwell's fleshy face turned to abject fear when he realized who was inside the tent with him—alone, at that.

"You! Boone, listen, I—I mean, are you mad? What gold?"

"I'm mad, all right, and you can slice that word either way, it'll cut true."

Dan'l had learned years ago to read faces close for the clues. Birdwell's was the worst type of all, in Dan'l's experience: shrewd eyes and a sly, hard mouth. It was the mouth that always showed softness or meanness in a man. And this mouth was as mean as they came.

So Dan'l didn't trifle with it. He growled impatiently and slapped his muzzle against Birdwell's skull a good crack, knocking the powdered wig askew.

"Damn you, Birdwell, if I was ever tempted to kill a man in cold blood . . . don't try to fox me, you thievin' son of Lucifer, or I'll leave you deader 'n last Christmas! Break out that damn gold, and mister, I mean hump it *quick*!"

151

He slapped Birdwell again with the butt, and by now this show of brute force had put fear in Birdwell's eyes. However, the man's greed surpassed even his cowardice. He couldn't stop himself from protesting in a whining, nasal voice:

"But that money is now revenue of the Colony of Virginia, owed to the treasury. I can't—"

"Pipe down, you thieving Tory! You're fixen to drive us out *and* steal our money. I played it your way long enough. Now, by the living Jesus, *I'm* making the medicine around here and you're taking it. Hand over them shiners, or get set to shovel coal in Hell!"

"No, *you* go to Hell, Boone, you stinking piece of offal!"

Enis Birdwell, as a surprised Dan'l found out in an eyeblink, was a quick man despite his prodigious, pear-shaped bulk. Bridwell had put both hands up obediently when Dan'l got the drop on him. Too obediently, and that should have caught Dan'l's notice.

For as Dan'l found out a moment later, the crafty administrator carried a tiny but deadly "muff gun"—a single-shot, .32-caliber flintlock pistol barely bigger than a man's palm—inside the collar of his doublet. It was a simple matter to slip it out behind his head and get the drop on his surprised captor.

But luckily, Dan'l, too, was a fast man. The moment the gun appeared in Birdwell's pudgy fist, Dan'l ducked. Birdwell fired, and Dan'l felt the bullet hum past his ear with a blowfly drone.

But though Dan'l was still alive, the entire damned army had just been alerted!

"Don't kill me, Boone!" Birdwell begged, his eyes bulging in fear like wet, white marbles. "You'll never get that gold if you do, it's too well hidden!"

Dan'l cursed, for he believed the tight-fisted bastard. Dan'l had no time for anything but saving his own skin if he could. Already he could hear feet pounding toward the front of Birdwell's tent, and sergeants shouting orders.

Dan'l smashed his rifle stock into Birdwell's left temple, and the man collapsed as if his bones had turned to jelly. In a heartbeat, Dan'l had his knife to hand and was slashing his way out the back of the tent.

Dan'l had a few seconds of grace because of his stolen uniform—the confused troopers held their fire, at first, as the big frontiersman raced back toward Jip's position near the tree line.

But Dan'l, despite being a fleet-footed sprinter, still had plenty of open ground to cover when somebody screamed the command to open fire.

"Jip!" he roared. "Head back to the main formation!"

But Jip stubbornly took cover behind a log and brought his muzzle to the ready, covering his old chum's sitter. The next moment, all hell busted loose around both men. Line after line of redcoat troops opened fire on the fleeing man, and lead balls rained in like deadly hail. Divots of grass and soil were torn loose, branches snapped off all around both men.

"Katy Christ!" Jip roared out, so scared he had to make noise to see if he was alive.

Dan'l considered it nothing less than a miracle when he hit the tree line without being shot. But even as he hurtled to temporary safety, he felt a sharp tug under his left armpit. Dan'l glanced down and saw a flint-tipped arrow protruding from the stolen tunic.

He glanced over his shoulder at a distant ridge and realized—not only had the mighty Sheltowee failed to get that gold, but War Hawk still meant to kill him.

Cussing, Dan'l pushed all that from his mind and followed Jip back to their hobbled mounts. War Hawk, Birdwell, and that gold would have to wait—right now there was a more pressing battle to fight.

Chapter Nineteen

"Target!" Jip called triumphantly as Dan'l's flint-lock roared, and yet another Brit fusilier folded to the ground.

Jip, lying in a prone position about ten yards from Dan'l, discharged his musket and dropped another redcoat.

"Move up!" Dan'l ordered, slinging his rifle and springing onto his horse's back. Quickly, the two trailsmen rode on ahead of the marching formation and again took up positions in the trees.

It had never occurred to either Dan'l or Jip to ride straight back and join their men at Dick's River. Instead, knowing well how the British infantry always operated, the two friends turned into roving skirmishers.

Dan'l referred to what he was doing now as "thinning out the flanks" during a march. The British had a peculiar obstinacy: Once the attack order was given, a sacred inevitability took over. They *would* not break ranks, come Hell or high water. In the open fields of Europe, such a battle style was formidable; here in the densely forested New World, however, it was suicidal.

Soldier after soldier dropped as the two hustling Kaintucks evened the odds a bit for their waiting force. Dan'l also hoped it was unstringing some British nerves. He had faith in the courage of his Kentucky Rifles, but few of the men were combat veterans. Dan'l had to give his men a fighting chance.

Now and then, the harried redcoats fired back while on the march, a surprise volley that sent a wall of lead screaming at Dan'l and Jip. Both men had bruised faces from flying chunks of bark.

"King George's *girls!*" Jip taunted them after yet another volley ruined a dozen trees but left him and Dan'l breathing. "Buncha damned pusguts playin' at soljers!"

"Caulk up," Dan'l snapped at the old Irishman. "Just keep holding and squeezing, old campaigner. Five more minutes, and these little tin bastards will reach Dick's River."

War Hawk, safe on a timbered ridge overlooking the valley, liked what he was seeing. How Boone could have survived that rock slide back in Sioux country, only the Wendigo could know. But War Hawk still refused to accept the "immortality" claims about Boone. No man's clover was that deep. And it looked as if Sheltowee's was about to run out soon now.

But a voice like a gnawing worm worked in his head: *Twice you left him for dead. Is it luck or big medicine?*

War Hawk shook off such thoughts and again studied events below. Nothing could be more useful to the Indians than bloody battles between the hair-faces. How War Hawk had rejoiced when the French and English faced off for nine long years! And clearly, another white man's clash was building right now.

From his present vantage point, War Hawk could see all of it below like a sand painting: the huge formation of redcoat warriors, bayonets glinting in the new sun as they advanced to the west; Sheltowee and his hoary-headed companion, desperately sniping from the flanks; and the local settlers massed at Dick's River, waiting for the beef-eaters to arrive and annihilate them with their superior numbers and training.

War Hawk's pox-scarred face eased into a wide smile when he noticed something else. Enis Birdwell was now hastily saddling his horse.

A bloody rag was tied around Birdwell's head, and he staggered a bit as he wrestled those gold-laden panniers across his horse.

War Hawk watched Birdwell ride out from the encampment below, bearing due east toward Virginia. That meant he would cross this very ridge on his way to the Old Colonial Pike.

That gold, War Hawk realized, was of infinite value to the whiteskins. It had already enriched War Hawk once—why not again?

War Hawk shoved a tomahawk into his clout and covered it with his beaded leather shirt. Then he walked down from his cave atop the ridge to the trail Birdwell would take.

Now and then, as he waited, War Hawk heard Boone and the old man's guns roaring, the noise steadily receding as they approached the river. The Shawnee felt a sting of familiar disappointment when he realized that Boone would not likely survive this bloodbath that was building to its climax. That meant War Hawk would be deprived of the pleasure of killing him and stealing his final breath.

But if so, War Hawk was determined to at least obtain Boone's head. It could be packed in brine, like a buffalo tongue, and put on display for every Indian to see.

War Hawk's pleasant reverie was interrupted when Birdwell's big sorrel suddenly rounded a shoulder of the ridge.

The white man wore a brace of pistols. But War Hawk, smiling at him, brandished no weapons. Birdwell's surprise quickly turned into irritation.

"What is it?" he demanded impatiently.

"Careful of the body in the trail," War Hawk replied helpfully.

"What body?" Birdwell looked around impatiently.

"Right there," War Hawk replied, pointing beside Birdwell's horse. While the revenue officer stared, his face perplexed, War Hawk moved quick as a darting minnow. The tomahawk twirled end-over-end, slicing hard into Birdwell's abdomen.

Birdwell watched his own blood come out in gouts as thick as ropes. With a strangled cry, he dropped from the saddle like a dead weight and landed in a heap in the trail—precisely where War Hawk had pointed.

The Shawnee removed the panniers of gold. Then he stripped the horse of its rigging and used one of Birdwell's pistols to shoot the animal in the head. War Hawk never stole a horse from cowards, only warriors, for theirs were the best mounts.

Chances were good that Boone could never survive this looming battle. But he had survived others, and if he lived this time, the dead Birdwell would send a strong challenge: If Sheltowee wanted those glitter coins again, he'd have to come after them.

"That's it, Jip!" Dan'l shouted to his friend. "Now we ride forward and pitch into the fight!"

Dan'l had lost count of how many men he and Jip had taken out. But the British force still looked formidable as they began to file out onto the east bank of Dick's River.

So far, Evan was holding up like a veteran

campaigner. It was critical—in battles with one-shot weapons—that firing discipline be maintained above all else. "Wild shots" and firing too soon could instantly sink an entire army. But Evan was moving steadily up and down the firing line, calming the men, even joking with them, urging them to hold fire a bit longer until hits were assured.

"Column of files!" shouted a redcoat sergeant. "Full front . . . face!"

Like a well-oiled mechanism, the British juggernaut wheeled around into firing position.

"Port . . . *arms*! Forward . . . *march*! Hep . . . hep . . . hep!"

Steadily, advancing in perfect cadence, the redcoats headed across the gravel bar. By now Dan'l and Jip had fled across the river and joined their men.

"Front rank cover down better!" Dan'l roared out. "Let them fire first, and take the brunt of it. Then shoot back before they can recharge!"

The confident British commander ordered the first volley while his men were halfway across the shallow creek. Dan'l cried out in dismay when a score of Kaintucks—Morgan Trapp and Nat Bischoff among them—folded to the ground clutching wounds. Dan'l and Jip instinctively moved to reinforce the weakest point on the line.

"Fire at will!" Evan and Dan'l roared out repeatedly, and now redcoats, too, began to drop as fire was returned, though not in one volley. But the British, knowing nothing of that fifty-man reserve force back in the trees, sniffed victory and pushed carelessly closer.

"Second platoon!" Dan'l shouted. "On the line and fire!"

A victory cry rose up from the deluded British. A second later, fifty Kentucky marksmen stepped out from the trees and fired over the heads of their kneeling companions. In an eyeblink, the British force was thinned out drastically. And with the first Kaintuck platoon now reloaded, Dan'l wasn't at all surprised to hear the Brit commander shout out desperately: "Cease fire, cease bloody fire! We surrender!"

A powerful huzzah rose from the victorious Kaintucks as they swept forward to disarm the invading troopers before they could pull a fox play.

Evan, who had received a slight wound, tossed his hat into the air and whooped. "We done 'er, Dan'l! By God, we *done* 'er. The Kentucky Rifles held!"

A grin divided Dan'l's bruised, powder-blackened face. Years from now, when these men bounced their grandkids on their knees, they would proudly recount their part in the glorious Gravel Ford Scrape, as it came to be known.

But for right now, Dan'l knew the battle wasn't quite over. Not so long as Enis Birdwell roamed free—and had that stolen gold with him.

Jip, busy stacking confiscated British rifles in piles, watched Dan'l swing up onto Rip and rein back around toward the settlement.

"I know you're on Birdwell's spoor," Jip told his friend. "And a damned pismire needn't be a-scairt of Birdwell. But take it from this old Injin killer, Dan'l. It's that murdering son of a bitch War Hawk you best watch out for."

Chapter Twenty

Birdwell and his horse were gone by the time Dan'l returned to the common square. But the trail was easy to follow. Dan'l could tell, from the depth of the rear hoofprints, that Birdwell was carrying the gold. Dan'l set out on the revenue officer's trail, dividing his attention between the ground in front of him and the terrain surrounding him.

An owl abruptly hooted, and Dan'l reined in his ginger.

Boone sat his saddle for a long time, listening to the young day. The "owl" hooted again, from a different direction. So War Hawk already had him in sight? And now he was waging his familiar war of nerves.

The noise from the surrender at Dick's River

had finally faded behind Dan'l, absorbed by the thick forest. Boone made sure, first, where the bird chatter was and was not evident. Then, his eyes in constant motion, he clucked to his horse.

Dan'l already knew, from guesswork and logical deduction, that War Hawk was holed up somewhere on this long ridge. He also knew War Hawk was like a crisis fever: He must be faced, and he *must* be whipped, or the Kaintucks would be burying their women and children early for years to come.

Dan'l also realized, the moment he found Birdwell's body, that War Hawk again had that gold.

The blood staining Birdwell's shattered abdomen was only tacky—not yet clotted. Sweat eased out from Dan'l's hairline as he realized how close the Shawnee must be.

"Scalper of children!" Dan'l called out. "This is one kill I do not begrudge you! Birdwell deserved a hard death and got one. But leave that gold behind and run now if you wish to live!"

This provoked a mocking loon-laugh. Dan'l, his back to the bole of a tree, his flintlock pistol to hand, desperately tried to locate the sound. But War Hawk was an expert at "throwing" his voice from seemingly any direction.

"Run!" Dan'l taunted. "I will not kill a fleeing woman. Leave that gold here, and I will leave your scalp on your head."

Again the owl hoot sounded. Hoping his own ears were accurate, Dan'l aimed for the one spot where the insects seemed unnaturally quiet. On his way, he quickly picked up stones and flipped them off to the left, making noise closer to the trail.

His deception worked. Dan'l rounded a tangled deadfall, walking silently on his heels, and there lay War Hawk, watching in the opposite direction.

Dan'l could have shot him right then, a mere twitch on the trigger to send that red bastard to Indian Hell. But despite War Hawk's abominable crimes, Dan'l couldn't sink to his pagan level of morals.

"Stand up, child-killer," Dan'l ordered.

War Hawk twitched violently, then whirled around. But the single, staring eye of Boone's rifle muzzle persuaded him to leave his weapons where they lay.

Dan'l spotted the panniers nearby. "I said stand up," he repeated calmly.

"Why? I'll only fall back down here after you shoot me, Sheltowee. I think I'll stay right here."

Dan'l fired, and War Hawk flinched violently again. But Boone had deliberately missed. Now he tossed his rifle to one side.

"Stand up," Dan'l repeated, unsheathing the knife that the Sioux girl had given to him in White Bear's camp. "And help me tie your left wrist to mine."

When he understood what was happening, the incredulous War Hawk tossed back his head and laughed wildly. "Boone, your 'nobility' has just cost you your entrails! I will cut you open from throat to rump!"

Both men left their knives stuck in the ground while they used their right hands to lash their left wrists together with rawhide.

"After I gut you, Boone," War Hawk taunted, "it will be the same for your family. After I top your woman."

"Ready?" said Dan'l, ignoring the taunts.

War Hawk nodded. Keeping a wary eye on each other, both men squatted and gripped their knives.

"Now!" Dan'l said, and the struggle was on.

Dan'l had more muscle than War Hawk, and better wrestling skills. But Dan'l was also in poor fettle, still healing from his burns. So he knew he couldn't hope to win a protracted fight.

They got their knives free at the same moment, and Dan'l instantly went for a wrestler's takedown, dropping backward and wrapping his legs around War Hawk's ankles to topple him. It worked, but their lashed wrists prevented Dan'l from getting into position for a killing thrust. He only managed a good slash across War Hawk's chest.

The Shawnee countered with a furious, slashing attack that repeatedly cut Dan'l. But War Hawk, too, was unable to get leverage or position for a killing blow without exposing himself to a killing thrust. With only one hand to use, a man had to depend on many smaller cuts to weaken his opponent.

Both men scrambled to their feet, each taking

a breather but never losing sight of the knife in his opponent's hand.

"You tried to win quick, Sheltowee," War Hawk taunted him. "But you failed. Now the game is mine, immortal one!"

Dan'l was forced to use his right forearm to block the next series of attack thrusts. But while War Hawk was still taunting him, Dan'l brought his right knee up hard into the Shawnee's crotch. War Hawk sucked in a hissing breath, and his eyes glazed over for a moment.

In that instant when War Hawk's nerves were paralyzed from Dan'l's blow, the big frontiersman made his move. He cocked his right arm out level with War Hawk's neck and thrust hard, instantly severing the huge carotid artery. But Dan'l's blade went even deeper, puncturing the windpipe and raising a horrid, gurgling scream of pain from his foe.

War Hawk dropped his knife, choking on his own blood, and sank to his knees. In a heartbeat, Dan'l had severed the rawhide and stood triumphantly over his vanquished foe.

Dan'l did not gloat or torment his enemy. But a quiet, unpitying satisfaction filled him as he stood there for the next few minutes, watching War Hawk's miserable death agony. Each gasping breath sucked blood into his lungs, and finally he died of drowning on dry land.

Dan'l recruited his horse, and then loaded that gold over the ginger's rump. First he meant to visit his family, make sure they were all right. Then Dan'l was going to look up Judge Josiah

Burns and turn that gold over to him.

Boone looked at the dead renegade and realized. Only two things bound a man to duty in this world, family and honor. War Hawk had respected neither. And he had died as miserable and lonely as he had deserved.

"C'mon, boy," Dan'l called out wearily to his horse, "let's go home."

DAN'L BOONE

DODGE TYLER

THE KAINTUCKS

The Natchez Trace is the trail of choice for frontiersmen heading north from New Orleans. But for Dan'l Boone and his small band of boatmen, the trail leads straight into danger. Lying in wait for the legendary guide is a band of French land pirates out for the payroll he is protecting. And with the cutthroats is a vicious war party of Chickasaw braves out for much more—Dan'l Boone's blood!

___4466-8 $3.99 US/$4.99 CAN

DAN'L BOONE

WARRIOR'S TRACE
Dodge Tyler

The Kentucky River has long been the lifeblood of American settlers near Dan'l Boone's home of Boonesborough. But suddenly it is running red with blood of another kind. The Shawnee and the Fox tribe have joined together in an unprecedented war to drive the white man out of their lands once and for all. And if Dan'l can't whip the desperate settlers into a mighty fighting force soon, he—and all of Boonesborough—might not survive the next attack.

___4421-8 $3.99 US/$4.99 CAN

Dorchester Publishing Co., Inc.
P.O. Box 6640
Wayne, PA 19087-8640

Please add $1.75 for shipping and handling for the first book and $.50 for each book thereafter. NY, NYC, and PA residents, please add appropriate sales tax. No cash, stamps, or C.O.D.s. All orders shipped within 6 weeks via postal service book rate. Canadian orders require $2.00 extra postage and must be paid in U.S. dollars through a U.S. banking facility.

Name_____
Address_____
City_____State_____Zip_____
I have enclosed $_____ in payment for the checked book(s).
Payment <u>must</u> accompany all orders. ❑ Please send a free catalog.
CHECK OUT OUR WEBSITE! www.dorchesterpub.com

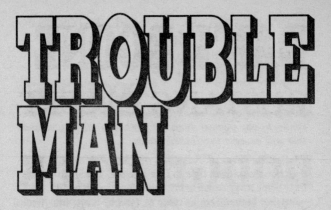

TROUBLE MAN

ED GORMAN

Ray Coyle used to be a gunfighter. And when he gets word
his boy has been killed in a gunfight in Coopersville, he has
to go there—to bring the body home. But when the old
gunfighter steps off the train, he brings his gun with him,
along with something else . . . trouble.

___4440-4 $4.99 US/$5.99 CAN

KIT CARSON

KEELBOAT CARNAGE
DOUG HAWKINS

The untamed frontier is filled with dangers of all kinds—both natural and man-made—dangers that only the bravest can survive. And so far Kit Carson has survived them all. But when he sets out north along the Missouri River he has no idea what lies ahead. He can't know that the Blackfeet are out to turn the river red with blood. And when he hitches a ride on a riverboat, he can't know that keelboat pirates are waiting just around the bend!

___4411-0 $3.99 US/$4.99 CAN

BLOOD HUNT

David Thompson

With only his oldest friend and his trusty long rifle for company, Davy Crockett explores the wild frontier looking for adventure, and has the strength and cunning to face any enemy. But even he may have met his match when he gets caught between two warring tribes on one side and a dangerous band of white men on the other—all of them willing to die—and kill—for a group of stolen women. It is up to Crockett to save the women, his friend and his own hide if he wants to live to explore another day.

_4229-0 $3.99 US/$4.99 CAN

Dorchester Publishing Co., Inc.
P.O. Box 6640
Wayne, PA 19087-8640

Please add $1.75 for shipping and handling for the first book and $.50 for each book thereafter. NY, NYC, and PA residents, please add appropriate sales tax. No cash, stamps, or C.O.D.s. All orders shipped within 6 weeks via postal service book rate. Canadian orders require $2.00 extra postage and must be paid in U.S. dollars through a U.S. banking facility.

Name_____
Address_____
City_____ State_____ Zip_____
I have enclosed $_____ in payment for the checked book(s).
Payment <u>must</u> accompany all orders. ❑ Please send a free catalog.